CRANE HOCKEY

ONE *pucking* WISH

USA TODAY BESTSELLING AUTHOR
ELLIE WADE

To all my snowed-in, forced proximity, enemies to lovers, hockey-loving romance fans. This one is for you.

And, to the show FRIENDS—thank you for being my therapy for the past thirty years.

CHAPTER ONE

PENELOPE

Gabby chatters away. She's one of the rare people in the world who still enjoys talking on the phone. I'd prefer a text or email from my high school best friend. Seeing that I speak to her twice a year, I guess I can't complain. We're eight years removed from our best-friends-forever status. Yet she's always quick to include me when there's any gossip she thinks I may be interested in.

After graduation, we grew apart. I went off to college, and she stayed in the small, one-blinking-red-stoplight town we grew up in. I don't understand it since I couldn't wait to leave that place. It always felt so small and suffocating. Then again, Gabby and I had very different home lives. While she was raised by two doting, happily married parents, I grew up with a single mother who was an alcoholic to boot. My entire goal in life was to escape.

My former best friend is a decent enough person—we just have nothing in common anymore except our past. Rest assured, anything pertaining to said past will spark a call from her whether I want it or not. Today, the news definitely falls in the not category. In fact, the gossip she's going on about isn't, in fact, news to me. I've been staring at the social media post of the engagement announcement for several hours now.

"Can you believe he's engaged?" she asks, and though I can't see her, I can imagine her big green eyes bugging out of her head right now. She's always been somewhat of a drama queen.

"Yeah, I know. It's crazy. I'm happy for him," I lie through my teeth because the truth is, I'm not remotely happy for him. I'm jealous and heartbroken. Once upon a time, he promised that the only finger he'd put a ring on was mine.

It's ridiculous to hold him to something he said nine years ago, but I do.

"Yeah, she's a model. I guess she's been in like two Target ads," Gabby exclaims.

"Wow. That's pretty cool."

More lies.

I hate the girl. I don't think the fact that she's a model is cool at all.

Gabby continues yapping. I half-heartedly listen as I scroll through the engagement pictures of the love of my life on social media, as I have been for hours now. Everything about the photos shatters my heart, but I can't look away. He looks so happy, and it hurts. But maybe the most painful realization is she's literally everything I'm not.

She's tall and thin, while I'm average at five foot five inches and on the curvy side. In fact, according to the sizing charts in the stores, I'm considered plus-sized. She has long dark brown, almost black hair while I have a deep red. Her skin is evenly toned and tan. Mine is pale as a ghost with freckles. It's as if he searched for someone the exact opposite of me.

"I guess her parents are from Mexico, and she comes from a lot of money. Her father owns some company down there, but I can't remember what it was...maybe textiles or something with investments?" Gabby continues.

"Those are two very different things," I say.

"It doesn't matter. The point is she's rich or at least her parents are. I heard the wedding is going to be amazing. Are you going? You and Tucker are still friends, right?"

"Uh, you know… not really. I haven't spoken to him in a while. I'm probably not invited."

"Are you kidding?" Gabby gasps. "I heard they're going to invite everyone from our class. The wedding is going to be huge. I'm sure you are. You and Tucker have been friends since third grade."

Considering we graduated with forty-five people, inviting them all wouldn't make a massive guest list. Even if everyone brought a date, that would only be ninety people. I wouldn't be surprised if Tucker invited our whole graduating class. He was friends with everyone and voted the most popular, funniest, nicest, and most likely to succeed. Yeah, in our tiny little town, Tucker Fenway was a god… and he was mine.

As it goes in small towns, there wasn't a time in my life when I don't remember Tucker being a part of it. However, in third grade, we truly became inseparable. We were assigned seats next to one another, and I helped him cheat on his spelling test. Even at eight years old, I was smitten. He and I organized a "king of the hill" group and proceeded to play that specific game every recess of that year, solidifying our best friend status. It was over after that. We were besties throughout the rest of elementary and middle school. In the fall of freshman year in high school, he asked me to the homecoming dance. That night ended in a kiss, igniting our perfect best friends-to-lovers fairy tale. Tucker and I dated throughout high school. We were the *it* couple and voted most likely to get married.

The truth is, I was nothing without Tucker. He put me on the map and made me somebody in that town of nobodies. He was charming and charismatic. Everyone loved him, and by extension, they loved me, too. Because he loved me. Without him, I was just the daughter of the town drunk. With him, I was high school royalty—as regal as one can be in that pathetic excuse for a high school.

"Are you going to bring a date?" she asks.

The picture of the supermodel holding out her hand to the camera, the flashy diamond on display as Tucker kisses her cheek, makes me feel ill.

"What?"

"To the wedding? Penelope Stellars, you cannot blow this off like you did our reunion. Everyone will be there!" Gabby chastises.

"I'm not blowing off anything," I sigh, my invisible Pinocchio nose extending farther.

"Well, are you dating anyone? If not, you can come by yourself. Promise you'll come, Penny. You haven't been back since your mom died. We all miss you."

I doubt that.

I clear my throat. "You know what? I really have to

finish some work stuff tonight, so I have to get going. But thanks so much for the call, Gabs. It was great talking to you." I work to make my tone sound sincere.

"Oh, okay. I mean, they haven't even set a date. I guess we can figure out everything after our invitations come," she says.

"Absolutely! Talk to you later." I don't recognize my own voice. The forced cheerfulness is nauseating.

I hit the red end button and drop it on the sofa. My gaze zeros back in on my laptop screen, where Tucker's sickenly blissful face stares back at me. I know I should be happy for him. He's a good person who deserves to find love.

It's my fault, really. All of it. I have no right to be upset.

Upon graduation, Tucker left for boot camp and the Army base in Texas, where he would be for several years. I headed up north to Central Michigan University, where I received a scholarship for school. I convinced him it wouldn't be fair for us to continue a long-distance relationship. I made the argument for breaking up and finding our paths with the understanding that we were meant to be together and we'd find our way back to one another.

He was devastated and promised me he could never love another. I felt the same way. Yet I just didn't see how pining for him from hundreds of miles away, for years, would help either of us. I was serious about making something of myself, terrified to live even a fraction of the life my mother had. Unlike her, I would do great things and be somebody of importance. Tucker was already important, but I knew he'd rise to the top of his unit and make a real difference in the Army. Both paths would be harder if we were tied to one another. It was the time in our lives to be selfish and put our needs first. When we accomplished our goals, we'd come back together.

This idea never scared me because I was so certain that Tucker was the man I was meant to spend the rest of my life with. He was positive, too, and swore that when he slid a ring on someone's finger someday, it would be mine.

So we went our separate ways the summer after high school graduation. It was difficult at first, and we talked on the phone all the time and texted constantly, but we were eventually able to slow our communication until it was a rarity.

For the first time in my life, I was free. I wasn't being pulled down by my mother or held up by Tucker. I was making my way on my own, solely on my efforts, and it was liberating.

Up until this point, I'd survived off coffee and

cheap boxed pastas. College brought the all-you-can-eat buffet in the cafeteria and happiness, which led to the freshman fifteen. I wasn't worried because I'd always been too thin and on the verge of malnourishment anyway. But sophomore year brought another fifteen and junior year another.

When I graduated from college, I was sixty pounds heavier than I was in high school. I went from a rail-thin teenager to a woman with major curves. The newfound breasts and ass, while a little obnoxious, weren't awful, but when I looked in the mirror, I didn't recognize myself.

Five years after the summer Tucker and I said our goodbyes, our class of forty-five, now twenty-three-year-olds, decided to get together for a five-year reunion of sorts. The get-together consisted of meeting at the local bar. Our town didn't have a grocery store, but it certainly had a bar. I knew Tucker would be there. I was sure he'd kept in touch with over half our graduating class, whereas I'd only spoken to Gabby and rarely. I had no desire to see forty-three of the people there, only one. Only him. But I felt ashamed for gaining so much weight. I dieted, barely eating anything but chicken breasts and broccoli the entire month prior to the reunion, and I lost four pounds of what was nothing more than water weight. My clothes didn't get any looser, and the reflection that met me in the mirror didn't change.

I went back and forth, deciding what to do, but ultimately, I couldn't go. I couldn't let my grand reunion with Tucker happen until I lost weight. I spent the whole evening stalking my classmates' social media, and sure enough, Tucker was there, beautiful as ever. My heart broke at missing my chance to see him. But I literally couldn't make myself go. I was terrified of what he would think of me. What if he wasn't attracted to me anymore? How would I have handled that rejection? It would've broken me.

That night, I promised myself that I'd lose the weight and I'd reach out to Tucker for our second chance. Yet another three years have passed, and I haven't lost the weight, nor have I seen Tucker in person. We've messaged via social media a few times over the years, but it's just been chitchat and nothing of importance.

Now, the love of my life is engaged, and if I'm being honest with myself, I won't go to his wedding either. I couldn't bear him looking at me with relief that he'd moved on.

In my day-to-day, my weight hasn't held me back. How many twenty-six-year-olds can say they're head of PR and social media for one of the most popular NHL teams in the country? I'm kick-ass at my job.

Even with the extra weight, I still feel pretty. I just don't feel like the girl Tucker loved anymore, and because of it, I've lost him—for good.

Even if I had still been skinny and had gone to that reunion, we might not have gotten back together. I have no doubt we both had changed since high school. But I'll never know.

My heart still yearns for him, yet I'm terrified that I blew my one chance at my happily ever after, all because I didn't have the confidence to put myself out there. Did I expect him to wait for me forever? Of course not. I guess I assumed that our love was strong enough that he'd be waiting for me when I was finally ready.

But no. He decided to go fall in love with a super-model instead.

Or, at the very least, a Target model.

My phone buzzes, and I look down to see a text from Iris. She's the wife of one of the starting forwards for the Cranes and also works under me as our social media and party planner. She's been in that position for a year now, and we've developed a friendship. Only this isn't a text between friends. It's work-related.

> We have a situation at The Station.

She mentions the local bar where the team likes to

party. I wasn't aware of any celebrating tonight since it's an off day. The team had practice and lifting earlier but no game, which is when they like to go out together.

My blood boils.

> Oh my God. What?

While I'm very good at my job, I can't deny I often feel like a glorified babysitter. It's ironic that I spent my life cleaning up my mother's messes and covering for her with the school and the other parents so that Child Protective Services wouldn't be called. And while a bunch of partying, testosterone-filled men drinking and celebrating is very different from dealing with someone with a legitimate disease and problem—they do bear striking similarities.

> There's just a little misunderstanding.
> Don't worry too much. Just come.

> Don't worry? Of course I'm worrying.
> What happened?

> Nothing serious. Simply something
> that needs your expertise.

That means something bad has happened. My blood begins to boil as angry tears fill my eyes. I just wanted one night to wallow in my heartache. Maybe eat a pint of ice cream and watch some *Friends*. But no… I have to go deal with grown-ass men who act like high schoolers.

It's Gunner. Isn't it?

Don't rush. It's not an emergency.
Drive safe. Just please come.

Gunner Dreven, the Cranes huge goalie, is a constant thorn in my side. Iris's lack of response tells me exactly what I need to know. He went off and did something foolish. Every time there is a problem, it's him… or at least fifty percent of the time.

Gunner, who the team refers to as Dreven or the Beast due to his massive size, is an asshole—plain and simple. I don't hate a lot of people. But I hate this guy.

Actually, maybe I do hate a lot of people.

Tonight alone, Target models and giant goalies are on my shit list.

It's just not a good night for me.

I'll be there soon.

I reply to Iris. Leaning my head back, I groan as it falls between my shoulders.

My red hair hangs loose in crazy wavy locks that

fall over my shoulders, and I have on a pair of baggy sweats and a T-shirt. None of which will do. When I first got this job, I found dealing with grumpy hockey players easier when I put on my power suit. Now, I won't go to work without my hair pulled back into a tight twist and a pant or skirt suit of some sort. Presenting myself this way makes me feel powerful, and when dealing with Gunner Dreven, that is a must. That man would eat me whole if I let him.

CHAPTER
TWO

GUNNER

Beckett, our team forward, called me to this bar, and now he's making me wait in the foyer. He gave some reason, but he was talking so fast I didn't even try to comprehend everything he said. I love the guy, but he's too much sometimes.

I can't say I'm pleased to be standing here. It's pissing me off if I'm honest. I had a perfectly respectable night of chilling at home planned. Which, with the intense season we've been having, is needed so I don't lose my ever-loving mind.

Not to mention, we're just coming off our bye week, which is always miserable. The entire team spent a week in Texas drinking, hanging out, and playing cards. It was a good time, as all bye weeks are, but getting back into the routine afterward is exhausting. My body needs as much downtime as I can get so it can perform the way I need it to.

I'll be thirty-three next week, which in my profession is pushing retirement age. I have no plans to retire anytime soon. As long as I take care of myself, I feel like that's a reasonable expectation. Yet standing out here in this drafty foyer with gusts of Michigan's winter winds streaming in below the entry door is making me both cold and cranky and isn't helping anyone.

Screw Beckett. Since when did I start listening to him?

I take a step toward the entrance to the bar when the exterior door swings open.

Penelope Stellars, the constant pain in my ass, rushes inside. Her eyes narrow when she sees me. "What did you do now, Dreven?"

"What the fuck are you talking about?" I furrow my brows.

"What did you do?" she repeats with a huff.

Closing my eyes, I pull in a breath through my nose to calm my building rage. Blowing up on this broad won't help anyone. I've learned that lesson. "Listen, Princess…"

"Don't call me that!" she protests, her voice a spine-chilling shriek. "It sounds like a dog's name, and I'm no poodle. You'll address me as Penelope or

Penny. Actually, you should probably call me Ms. Stellars."

I force out a laugh. "Yeah, *Penny*, I won't be calling you Ms. Anything."

She rolls her eyes. "Whatever, as long as you drop the stupid nickname, we're good. Now, what did you do?"

"Why do you keep asking me that?" The question comes out with a bit of a roar, and I don't miss the way Penny flinches.

She stands tall or attempts to. The woman is a foot shorter than my six-foot-five frame, but she can puff out her chest any day of the week. While, personally, I can't stand the woman, I can't deny that she has a nice rack. She has a nice body, period. Admittedly, I've dreamed of grabbing that ass of hers while she rode my cock. I'm not proud of that. I would've rather it had been about another woman, but my subconscious does what it wants.

While I may find her body attractive, nothing about her uptight, snooty personality turns me on. In fact, it does the opposite. She has such a stick up her ass, I don't know how she gets around. She's showing up at a bar wearing a tight black pencil skirt with a blazer. There's a hint of a blue flowy blouse under the blazer, but one wouldn't know with how she has that jacket buttoned up like a straitjacket. Her hair is pulled so tightly in some sort of twist on the back of her head that I'm sure it's giving her a headache. Who shows up to a casual bar dressed like she's ready for a press conference? She's obnoxious.

Penny opens her mouth to speak as the bar door opens, and Iris—the team's party planner and wife of our other forward, Cade Richards—pops her head into the foyer, wearing a pleased grin on her face. "Oh, good! You're both here."

"Iris…" Penny takes a step forward.

Iris backs away. Opening the door, she waves us in.

Moving a step back, I allow Penny to take the lead, and I follow her through the door. The bar is dark, and I squint in an attempt to see what's going on. As soon as we're firmly inside the bar, the door closes behind us, the lights flick on, and a rumble of "Surprise!" and Happy birthday!" reverberates through the space.

My gaze flicks to the entire team standing before us with what I can assume is a less-than-impressed expression. Each round wooden table has a bouquet of multicolored balloons. There's confetti, party hats, a huge-ass birthday cake, and way too much cheer for my taste.

I steal a glance toward Penny. A smile is plastered across her face, but I know her expressions well enough to know that it's fake as hell. She's just as uncomfortable as I am with all this attention.

Birthdays were never a big deal growing up. I think my mom realized that the less attention she brought to me, the happier my life would be. She never wanted to put me on the radar of the various men she dated over the years, and for good reason. My mom sure knew how to pick 'em. The revolving door of men coming in and out of our house consisted of deadbeats, sometimes drunks, oftentimes gamblers, and always abusive pricks.

The fact that I'm referred to as the Beast now is ironic because I spent most of my childhood and teenage years as a scrawny little rat. I'm what they called a late bloomer, not hitting my big growth spurt until I was damn near well out of high school. For eighteen years, I was skin and bones and easy bait for my mom's boyfriends. She conditioned me to hide, be quiet, and stay away.

There were no birthday celebrations to remind the jerks that there was someone else in the house they could beat on besides my mother. No, it was just a day like any other day, save for one minor detail. Each birthday before the current man sleeping in my mother's bed would wake, she would sneak into my room and wake me up with a kiss on my forehead.

"Happy birthday, my sweet boy," she would say.

She would ask me what my birthday wish was, and I would always say, "To be great at hockey," but I would always secretly wish, *"To grow strong enough to save you."*

She would then pull two donuts out of a bakery bag. They were always frosted in a bright hue and covered in sprinkles. It was the one time a year I ate a donut, and something about the birthday donut was next level.

I once asked her if all donuts were so delicious, and she said that birthday donuts were extra yummy because they were filled with birthday magic.

We would sit atop my bed and slowly eat our donuts. I'd savor every bite and every second where I could just be in the moment with my mom, happy and hopeful. There was a time when I actually believed that this birthday magic my mother spoke of was real, and I dreamed that it would eventually save us from our circumstances.

When the special treat was gone, she'd give me one more kiss on the forehead and sneak back out of my room as quietly as she had come in. And that was the entirety of my birthday celebration.

I made my secret wish every year for as long as I can remember, but in the end, I couldn't save her. Now, birthdays serve as another reminder of my failure. And, wouldn't you know, I share the day with one of my least favorite people.

"Our birthday isn't until next week," I grumble.

My protest does little to remove the smile from Iris's face. "I know, but we're going to be in Vancouver. We couldn't have a proper celebration so far from home, so we decided to throw you a party a little early. Plus, this way, it was really a surprise."

"Oh, it's definitely a surprise," Penny says through her forced grin.

Iris waves us forward. "Enjoy! We have lots of food, and of course everyone is here to celebrate you both. We'll cut the cake in a little bit." With a nod of her head, the music starts up, and it's a full-blown party.

Now that I understand what's going on, I realize Penny was probably called here under the guise of fixing some issue, and of course she thought said problem was me. Her questions from the foyer make complete sense.

I turn to her, narrowing my gaze. "I guess I didn't do anything now, did I?"

She rolls her eyes. "Oh, shut it," she says before heading toward the crowd of people waiting to celebrate us.

My birthday twin isn't fond of me, but I have to say the feeling is mutual.

Sebastian Calloway, our center, who we call Bash, hands me a bottle of beer. "Happy birthday, old man!"

"Cookie." I dip my chin in acknowledgment, using his other nickname, which he despises. The name is idiotic, and I feel like a complete jackass uttering the word, but Bash's adverse reaction brings me a little bit of joy every time.

His mouth falls into a frown, and he sighs. "Seriously? We agreed to let that go."

I shake my head. "I don't think so, and I'll be calling you a lot worse if you call me old again."

We have a pretty young team, and to someone like Bash, who just turned twenty-four, I might be considered older for this profession, but that doesn't mean I want to hear it. I'm sure I'm living in denial, but I plan on holding the starting goalie position for this team for years to come, provided my knees and hips hold out.

Bash waves his arm out in front of him, motioning to the scene before us. "Pretty cool, huh? Were you surprised?

"Cool? Not sure. Surprised? Yes."

"Aw, come on. What's better than all your best friends in one room celebrating the day you were born?"

The answer to that question is too vast to pinpoint a single response, so instead, I grunt and take a swig of my beer.

Bash slaps my bicep with a laugh. "The Beast in all his grumpy glory. Happy birthday." He clinks his beer bottle against mine. "I'm glad to be here celebrating with you."

"Thanks."

Everyone in the Cranes organization probably thinks of me as a family would of that one loner grumpy uncle at all the gatherings. They love me and are glad I'm here but don't know exactly what to do or say around me. The truth is, everyone here is my family—the only one I have. Despite the air I may put off, I love them all. I don't know where I'd be without this job or these people.

I've just never been what one would consider "a people person." When I was a child, I was conditioned to stay quiet and keep to myself. It was a matter of survival. Once I was in college, I found that attempting to change everything I've always been wasn't that easy. I grew up avoiding friendships and keeping to myself, which carried over into adulthood. It's quite difficult to be someone you're not, even if you may want to. Sometimes I think it'd be cool to be like others. Take our starting forward, for example. Cade is one of the coolest people I've met. The guy is as nice as can be and can talk to anyone. He could befriend a rock, if needed. Beckett is always the life of the party— fun, outgoing, and charming. It's rare not to see a smile on the dude's face. They are both so vastly different than I am. Even with an immense amount of effort, I could never be as outgoing as they are. And the truth is… I don't want to be. I'm pretty damn content being the more reserved, if not a little grumpy, one on the team.

As if my internal thoughts summoned him over, Beckett approaches wearing his classic shit-eating grin. "So on a scale of one to ten, how awesome was this year's bye week?" he asks.

"It was cool." I can't help but chuckle; the guy's charm penetrates even my thick skin.

"Right? Who needs house parties with a revolving door of women anyway? It's fun just to hang out together with our real friends."

"Mm-hmm." I smirk with a shake of my head.

Our bye week was different this time around. In years past, we rented a mansion in an exotic location and partied for a week straight. This year—thanks to the shortest courtship in history that led to Beckett's marriage to our team doctor—the week was more laid-back. Beckett has retired his whore ways and has settled into life as a married man. We still rented a mansion and had an abundance of food and alcohol, but it was more intimate. Those in attendance were family and friends of the team, not random hookups. We talked, hung out, and played cards. It was a great time.

"What?" Beckett raises a brow. "I just thought we could use a change of pace."

"Sure you did, Feltmore." I nod.

He huffs out a breath. "I did."

I'm just giving him a hard time. I'm happy he's found someone he wants to spend his life with. In my now almost thirty-three years of existence, I can honestly say that no one has come close for me.

The woman who stole his heart walks up to his side and supplies me with her brilliant smile. Our team doctor, Elena Cortez, recently turned Elena Feldmore, is a stunningly beautiful woman. I can see the appeal. As far as doctors go, she's pretty badass, too.

"Happy early birthday, Gunner." She's the only person here who calls me by my first name, and I like it.

Nicknames are fine among the guys, but when I step back and really think about it, being referred to as the Beast out in public is just weird.

"Thank you. I'm surprised you came out."

The team doc doesn't often join us at the bars after a game. It's not her scene.

"I wouldn't miss celebrating your birthday." She grins. "I won't stay out long. I'm still exhausted from all the fun we had last week. I'm waiting for that second trimester boost of energy to hit me, but this pregnancy has me exhausted."

Beckett wraps his hand around her waist and kisses her temple. When he leans back, he wears an expression of complete adoration.

Iris bounds over to our group. "It's cake time!"

She leads me to a high-top table with a sheet cake big enough to cover the entire surface. Penny stands facing our joint birthday cake, waiting. Begrudgingly, I step up to her side. All eyes in the place are on us as Iris lights the candles. I take calming breaths through my nose, wishing I were anywhere but here. All this attention on me is not my style.

Iris initiates the happy birthday song, and everyone in the place belts out the lyrics. I drown out the off-key melody, counting down the seconds until I can step out of the spotlight.

At the end of the song, Iris claps her hands together and cheers, "Make a wish!"

Her words crash a wave of nostalgia over me, and I freeze. Every muscle in my body goes stiff. Emotions that I haven't felt in so long weigh down on me. I feel everything as if I were still that frail little boy who had to sneak a sprinkled donut and a moment of his mother's time.

A squeeze of my hand pulls me from my memories, and I look down to see Penny.

"You okay?" There isn't an ounce of malice in her voice, and the way in which those two words soothe my rising panic unsettles me.

I pull in a breath and nod.

"On the count of three, make a wish and blow?"

I nod again.

Penny counts, "One, two." She looks at me with a reassuring grin, and it does something to me. I'm not used to being on the receiving end of her kindness. "Three."

She opens her mouth to blow and, with her eyes, directs me to do the same. I follow suit, and the pair of us extinguish the tiny flames of the candles. Right before the last candle is out, a vivid image comes to my mind. It's not a wish, exactly, but it's there in utter clarity, and if I'm honest, it freaks me the fuck out.

CHAPTER THREE

PENELOPE

Pulling my jacket tight around my middle, I scurry across the tarmac as what can only be described as ice snow pelts me in the face. I hate being cold. I should've gotten a job working for a Florida team. What possessed me to stay in Michigan is beyond me.

I hurry onto the plane and take a deep breath, relieved Mother Nature can no longer assault me. My cheeks burn, and I'm sure I look like a hot mess. My fair skin has always been overly sensitive. Undoubtedly, my cheeks will be tomato red the entire flight to Vancouver.

I find my usual seat toward the back as the rest of

the team files onto the plane. Opening my purse, I search for my compact to assess the damage. The pursuit is momentarily forgotten when a cup of coffee appears in my periphery. Not just any cup of coffee—a pumpkin spiced latte from Starbucks.

Dropping the compact into my purse, I take the paper cup from Iris, and a genuine smile finds my face. "Still?" I ask, already knowing the answer as the aroma of spices wafts through the air.

Iris takes the seat beside me and starts fiddling with her seat belt. "She says just a few more cups."

Taking a long sip of the heavenly goodness, I savor one of my favorite flavors. The fact that Iris has a hookup at the local Starbucks—who has somehow managed to sneak away a few bags of the mix to sell to her friends long after the pumpkin spiced latte is out of season—is not the sole reason I consider Iris one of my best friends. Admittedly, a year ago, my icy exterior softened toward her when she brought me my favorite drink—even though it could no longer be purchased. Now, Iris is one of my best friends and, honestly, one of my only friends.

Working so many hours with as many men as I do doesn't supply many opportunities to foster quality relationships with women. I don't have much time for a social life. If it were really important to me, I suppose

I could make time. But my life is my work. So it helps that one of the few women I get to work with is as cool as Iris.

I swallow down the warm coffee and sigh. "Really?"

Iris nods. "Yeah. She's almost sold out of the mix she stored away."

"And you have no other black market pumpkin spiced latte dealers?" I raise a brow, causing Iris to laugh.

"Unfortunately, no." She tightens her lap belt. "Can you believe the hail outside? Taking off in a storm like that is kind of freaking me out."

Hail. That's what it's called.

I lean my head back against the seat's headrest and release a chuckle. "Unbelievable," I mutter under my breath.

"What is?" Iris asked.

I turn toward her. "I've been referring to hail as ice snow all day. I've lived in Michigan my whole life, and I somehow completely forgot the word hail."

"It happens." Iris grins, and with a shrug, she states, "I mean, ice snow is pretty accurate, too."

Wrapping my hands around the warm cup of coffee, I hold it to my chest like a security blanket. "It's just been a weird week. I feel like I'm losing my mind."

"Anything you want to talk about?" Iris wears a face of real concern, and I almost want to open up to her.

I could tell her I've been obsessively looking at the post and pictures of the love of my life's engagement announcement to another woman on social media. I could tell her that my birthday tomorrow is sparking some kind of late quarter-life crisis, making me question every decision I've ever made. I could tell her that she's my closest friend, and it's not lost on me that our friendship is a hundred percent grounded in her feeding my coffee addiction. I could tell her that despite showing up every day and presenting myself as a badass businesswoman, I'm drowning in this feeling of mediocrity that I can't seem to escape from.

Instead, I opt to say, "Eh, it's nothing. Just normal work stuff."

"Well, if you need my help with something, let me know."

"I will." I force the corner of my lips to tilt up into what I hope is an authentic smile before taking another sip of my coffee.

"Penny?"

"Yeah?"

"I don't want to break up the love affair you have going with your pumpkin latte, but you should know you have a situation going on." Iris makes a circular motion in front of her face.

"I have something on my face?"

"Yeah, a little mascara from all the ice snow out there." She grins.

"Oh, I was just checking that when you sat down." I pull down the tray table and set my coffee down before retrieving the compact in my purse.

The reflection that stares back at me makes me gasp. I don't have a little something on my face. I have legitimate streaks of mascara streaming down my cheeks and black circles around my eyes, making me look like a deranged cousin of the Joker.

"What in the actual fuck? My new mascara claims to be smudge-proof and water-resistant. What is this mess? I look like a demon!" I whisper-hiss as not to bring unwanted attention my way. I can't let the guys see me like this. I'd never hear the end of it. Thankfully, our seats are in the back of the plane, and I've seemingly gone unnoticed.

Iris covers her mouth to hide a laugh.

The captain makes his announcement to stay seated, and the plane begins to taxi down the runway. A quick escape to the bathroom to clean up my face isn't in my immediate future, so I grab a makeup wipe from my carry-on and start wiping the mascara off my skin.

"You know, I went into the makeup store wanting to purchase the same brand I've worn since college, but no, you know how they always push the new products. I hate that overly spray-tanned Barbie talked me into switching. I knew better," I grumble as I pull the wipe across my face.

"It was the bag, wasn't it?" Iris eyes the new floral makeup bag in my lap.

I frown and roll my eyes. "Yes. I fell for the free-bag-with-purchase spiel. I'm embarrassed to be this weak."

"Hey, now. It's a gorgeous bag, and to be fair, the weather is pretty extreme. I'm sure your new mascara would work fine on a normal day."

Iris and I gasp in unison as the plane falls, and we lift from our seats. Priorities in place, I reach for my coffee to stop it from catapulting through the air. The seat belt across my lap pulls against my thighs, and the plane settles, continuing its ascent.

"I hate flying through storm clouds." Iris pulls the strap on her seat belt as tight as it will go.

"It'll be fine once we're through them. The air will be calmer above the clouds," I say to reassure myself as much as Iris. I have always found it fascinating how planes can fly above the clouds where the weather can be completely different than it is on land. "Anyway, tell me... how is married life treating you?"

"Perfect," Iris says with a dreamy sigh. One mention of her husband and she's seemingly forgotten her anxiety over the turbulent flight. "The best."

She married one of the Cranes starting forwards, Cade Richards, about five months ago. Cade had been her friend since she was eight years old, though they hadn't been as close in recent years. I wasn't on the team's bye-week vacation in Barbados last year, but that's where they rekindled their love affair. They are a sweet couple. Cade has always been one of my favorite guys on the team. Iris has another connection to the team, Cade's best friend—her brother, Beckett—the other starting forward who actually randomly married our new team doctor, Elena, in a secret Vegas wedding last summer about a month before Iris and Cade's wedding.

Now, that pairing was something I never saw coming, but I have to admit, they are really cute together. Elena is five months pregnant, and Beckett, our reformed one-night stand king, couldn't dote on her or love her more. He treats her like a goddess, and even my black heart can admit it's adorable.

"So Beck and Elena are still set on not finding out?" I ask, wanting to keep Iris's thoughts off the turbulence.

"Still set on having the sex of the baby be a surprise. I think Beckett would find out in a second if he could, but he'll do anything Elena wants. It's still so weird to see him like this, married and in love. It's like he's still himself but so different. You know?"

"Oh definitely. As I've told you, I always thought he'd be a bachelor for life or at least until his hockey days were over."

"I guess when you find the one, you just know. Love can find you when you're least expecting it." She nudges my leg with her own and shoots me a smile.

"I don't think so." I shake my head. "I don't have time or patience for a man."

"You will if it's the right one. You're a catch, Penelope Stellars. It's going to happen."

Bless her little heart, but she's delusional. "Not for me." I scoff. "My heart is locked down tight. I mean, nothing about being in a relationship remotely entices me. I just can't..." I scowl. "Plus, I'm quite sure you're the only person in the world who actually likes me."

"That's not true." She furrows her brows. "You may think you only emit bitch energy, but we all see right through that. Everyone likes you."

"Well, that's a shame."

Iris laughs. "Oh, Penny...drink your coffee."

We emerge from the storm clouds and settle into smooth flying on our way to Canada. Iris scrolls Pinterest boards, no doubt for inspiration on planning her next event, while I set up my compact and its tiny mirror on the little tray table. I've had enough of this funk I'm in. There's no longer any room for me at this pity party. I'm leaving it. Step one is to get my face back in order.

My new makeup may be shit, but it'll have to do. And at least I got a free bag out of it.

CHAPTER FOUR

GUNNER

The arena, dimly lit save for the intense lights shining on the ice, is deafening with the roar of the Vancouver fans. The tension crackles in the air, but it's not the welcome excitement that comes when we're about to score a win. It's the burning electricity that stings with an impending loss. The game's final minutes tick away, and we can't seem to get it right.

Weight is heavy on my shoulders thinking of the three goals I've allowed into my net. It happens, yet when our offense is off, the burden is harder to bear. I loathe losing. In fact, there is little I hate more in the world. Vancouver's forward rushes toward me, and his stick pushes the puck over the ice with precision. Watching his eyes, the movement of his body, and the angle of his stick, I visualize the shot he'll take. I don't move into position until his stick raises, ready to strike. I can't risk him changing course. He slaps the puck, and I'm already in place. Gloved hand extended, I stop it.

"Let's go!" I roar from the net. My teammates, in possession of the puck, zoom down the ice as seconds tick off the clock.

We're down by one with mere moments left on the clock. The best we can hope for is a tie, but that will get us to overtime, where we have a chance at a win.

To anyone else, Feldmore and Richards would appear to have it together as they pass the puck, but I see the hesitation there. Something's off. Cade Richards slaps the puck to our center, Sebastian Calloway, in a new play we've been honing this week. Calloway is in position, but I know before his stick slaps the puck that it's over. Some days, we have it, and some days, we don't. We've been off this entire game.

The buzzer sounds as the Vancouver goalie hits the puck away, securing the win. The sea of dark-blue-and-green jerseys in the stands goes wild, the sound deafening as they celebrate their hometown win.

The six of us wearing Crane jerseys stand on the ice motionless for a second, stunned. On paper, we had this game in the bag. Yet unpredictability is what makes this sport so fun. The Canucks played better tonight, plain and simple.

Defeated, we exit the ice and make our way to the locker room.

"Well, that fucking sucked," one of our defensemen, Jaden Lewis, grumbles.

"Let's just get out of here and to the bar. Forget this whole night ever happened," Maxwell Park, another defensemen, chimes in.

"Agreed," Beckett states.

"It just wasn't our night." Cade sighs.

Thankfully, the coach's post-game talk is short. We shower and change. Eddy, our equipment manager, collects our bags and equipment to return to the plane while the rest of us pile into cars and head toward a bar.

The bar scene in Vancouver is decent, not that it matters. As long as there is alcohol, our guys could have a blast anywhere. Undoubtedly, the drinks will be pouring tonight as we drown our sorrows. Or at least, most of them will. I'll be sticking to my two-drink limit. The temptation to drink until I don't remember the sixty minutes we sucked out on the ice is strong. But my reasons for not getting shit-faced are stronger.

Growing up with drunks in my house who pushed my mother around on any given night left me with the resolve to never be out of control. I know I'd never hurt a woman or become a drunk, but I don't want to be without my senses. The thought of not having a clear mind or being in control doesn't sit well with me.

The driver yammers about the snow on the short drive to the bar. I only half listen, the conversation doing little to keep my interest. It's winter, and we're in Canada, so it's bound to snow. Instead, my mind goes over every second of the game, figuring out the moments we messed up. It's the cruelest form of torture, really, since there's not a damn thing I can do to change it.

The car skids to a stop outside a faded sign that says *Frank's*. I'm not sure who chose our final destination, but I suppose it doesn't matter. Though *Frank's* is nothing special, the bar has drinks, which is all the guys care about.

Two beers go down entirely too quickly, and I sigh in irritation. Now, what am I supposed to do for the rest of our time here? The more the team drinks, the more annoying they become.

The moment she enters the bar, the air changes. I'm certain she's here, though I've yet to lay my eyes on her. Why must I be so attuned to the bane of my existence? Penelope Stellars drives me batshit crazy, yet instead of ignoring her, my mind has decided to be aware of every step she takes.

"Hey, boys," she says from behind me. I resist the

urge to turn around. "Tough loss. We're going to keep everything cool tonight, yes? Make my job easy?"

"Of course, Miss Penny. Would you expect anything less?" Beckett teases.

Penny scoffs. The sound causes my back to stiffen.

Unable to ignore her anymore, I toss a glance over my shoulder. "Princess," I say in greeting, which is met with a scowl and a roll of her eyes.

Bash shoves his arm past me, a shot glass in his hand. "Do a shot with us, Pen."

"I'm good. Thanks, though. I'll be around if anyone needs anything," she replies. I don't have to see her face to know that she gave each person standing around the circle a warning look.

I order a third beer because… I can. The two-beer rule is a self-imposed guideline, not a hard and fast rule. I have a feeling that this night will be long, so one more bottle is warranted.

When we arrived at *Frank's*, the mood was low, but it doesn't take long for everyone to be in good spirits. The conversations morph from depressing defeat to upbeat and jovial, as the guys normally are. Personality-wise, I'm definitely the most dull on the team, and I wear that badge with pride. If I'm being honest, I play with a bunch of idiots. Yet somehow each one of them seems to make their idiocy endearing. They have a way of making me feel at ease and accepted. They're my family, and despite being opposite of them all—they are the family I choose. I can't think of a better group of humans.

I've never been good with feelings, and I haven't vocalized any of this, but I feel it, and the connection I have with this group is so strong, it's undeniable. The first eighteen years of my life were pretty awful, but sometimes I can't help but think that the universe is making up for it with this chapter. Tonight's game aside, how many people can say they're living their ultimate dream with coworkers they cherish like family? It's pretty cool.

And, shit... that third beer is going to my head. I'm never this emotional, even in the safety of my own mind.

Giving my head a shake, I refocus on the conversation at hand.

"I just think it needs to be more than a once-a-year thing," Max states. "I can't wait until next year's bye week. I'm dreaming about them, for God's sake."

A boom of laughter sounds.

Bash shrugs. "It's not like I'll only make them once a year. I would make them at other times and bring them in. I'm just busy."

I realize they're lamenting over our second annual cookie competition at the resort we rented in Texas last month. Admittedly, Bash, our two-time winner, can bake a damn good cookie. This year, he entered with some chocolate and mint chip recipe he created. The cookies were incredible.

The competition started a couple of years ago at the bye week in Barbados. I don't remember how it came to be. One minute, we were all standing around talking, and the next, we were catching Ubers to the local supermarket for ingredients... well, they were. I don't bake. Bash made a chocolate chip cookie that was gooey and delicious with mini-chips that year, winning the competition and earning his team nickname, Cookie Monster, which we love to shorten to Cookie. He hates it. We find it hilarious.

Jaden leans in. "What do you mean you don't have time? You live alone with no pets or girlfriend. When you're not on the ice, you have all the time in the world. Bake us some damn cookies, Cookie."

Bash rolls his eyes. "Despite what you may think, I do have a life outside of this team."

"Doing what?" Beckett questions.

Bash avoids eye contact with Beckett and clears his throat. "I don't know. Hanging out with other friends."

Being the quiet one of the group, I'm somewhat of an observer, and I get the feeling that Bash is nervous.

"What friends?" Cade asks.

Bash shrugs. He moves the toe of his tennis shoe

against a spot on the floor. "Just friends. As stated, I have friends outside of you guys."

I don't doubt that's true. As the youngest member of the team, I'm sure he still keeps in contact with some of his college buddies.

"Well, tell these friends you're busy and make us some cookies. I'm dreaming about them, dude." Jaden takes a swig of his beer.

"I'll do my best," Bash responds.

"That's all I ask." Jaden grins.

Cade's thumbs move across the screen of his phone. He puts his phone in his back pocket and addresses the group. "Settle up with the bartender. We need to get back to the plane. I guess a storm is coming in, so Coach wants us in the air as soon as possible."

Penny rejoins our group. "Let's go, boys. We have to head out."

The guys disperse to pay their tabs.

"Tell Cade I'm outside grabbing us a car," Iris says to Penny.

"Okay, I'll be right out," Penny answers.

The guys head out of the bar. Only Penny, Jaden, Max, and me are left.

"What's taking so long?" Penny eyes the bar where Jaden is still paying his tab.

Max chuckles. "You know Jaden. The guy can talk

anyone's ear off. Go ahead and go. We're right behind you."

Penny's squinted stare darts between Max and me, uncertain.

"I promise we're good. We're seriously right behind you," he repeats.

"Okay, well, hurry and be safe."

"Will do." Max nods to Penny before turning to me. "I'm going to go get him."

I dip my chin in response, and my stare follows Penny as she heads to the exit. My focus veers to a table of obnoxious Canuck fans as the four guys watch Penny as she leaves.

The short one, who probably weighs no more than one hundred and twenty pounds soaking wet, sneers as Penny passes. He looks like some cracked-out version of a troll doll with his wispy bright blue wig. Turning back to his friends, he scoffs, "Why do only the ugly ones stay till close? Did you see her ass? That bitch would crush me."

His friends laugh, but I don't find him funny. Rage consumes me, and my vision blurs as I'm flooded with molten-hot anger. I can't think straight. My brain has ceased all functions. In fact, the only thing working is my fist as it finds his face.

CHAPTER
FIVE

PENELOPE

The drive from the bar to the airport is sure to take at least three years off my life. I don't remember so many winding roads driving to the rink for the game earlier. In fact, if my memory serves, the streets were fairly straight. Yet Julien, our cab driver, is sliding around these roads like nothing I've ever seen. I bet we've spent more time off the road than on it.

As I stare from the back seat out the front windshield, there isn't anything resembling a street in sight. Nothing is visible but blankets of white. "Is he even on the road?" I whisper to Iris.

The car fishtails, and Iris gasps, reaching out to grab my hand as my shoulder hits the back passenger door.

"Oh, don't you worry, ma'am." Our driver lifts his

chin and smiles at me through the rearview mirror. We're on the road alright."

Cade turns around and looks back at us from the front passenger seat. He gives us a reassuring look. "The airport is less than a mile away."

I know he meant it to be encouraging, but considering the way Julien drives, I'm not at all comforted.

"It must've snowed a good fifteen centimeters since we've been driving," Julien says.

"That's around six inches," Cade says over his shoulder.

"Thanks, smarty-pants, but I don't need a math lesson." I sigh, annoyed that I'm not already home safely in my bed.

Julien bobs his head. "They're predicting this will be the biggest storm since 1996. I wasn't born then, but I've heard stories of how we got over forty-five centimeters in one night."

Cade looks back and quirks a brow.

"Fine, tell me," I grumble.

"Around eighteen inches."

My eyes go wide. "You guys are supposed to get more than eighteen inches tonight? How did we not know about this? We need to fly out before we're stuck here."

"Oh, yeah, all the commercial flights are already being canceled," Julien states.

"Why didn't we leave earlier?" I look at Iris. The question is rhetorical. She doesn't have any more control over the schedule than I do. It just seems crazy that we didn't fly out right after the game.

Cade clutches the handle over the window as Julien slides around another corner. "I think we knew snow was coming, but for some reason, I don't think anyone realized it'd be this much."

"My grandma's been talking about it for days. She could feel it in her knees." Julien slows the vehicle as the airport comes into view.

"If only your grandma's knees could've communicated with our pilots." Iris attempts a joke, but her laugh falls flat when Julien plows over something, causing us to bounce in our seats.

"Did you just hit something?" The question comes out in a shriek.

Our driver shrugs. "I'm fairly certain it was nothing alive."

I lean my head back against the seat, close my eyes, and release a deep breath. Meditating seems like a solid plan. Surely, after a few deep breaths and some Zen, we'll be at the plane.

A yelp leaves my mouth and my butt lifts from the seat as Julien hits something else.

"Nothing to worry about," he reassures us.

I'm not convinced, but it doesn't matter because the team's plane is in view.

Oh, thank you.

I sigh in relief.

Julien pulls his car up next to an SUV parked several yards from the steps that lead up to the plane. I grumble a thank you and open my door as Cade no doubt gives Julien an excessive tip. In fairness, I couldn't drive much better, given these conditions. I'm just grateful to arrive in one piece.

A couple of the guys exit the SUV beside us and hurry up the plane steps. It's hard to make out who they are. With the amount of snow coming down, I can only see a few feet in front of my face.

Head down, I speed up the steps as fast as my three-inch heels allow. Cade and Iris follow me.

We board the plane to see Coach Albright, the pilot, and Jaden and Max talking in front of the cockpit.

"We have to go right now, or we'll be stuck here for the night," the pilot states.

I step toward them. "What is it?"

Jaden turns toward me. He and Max must've been the players in the SUV as snow still rests atop their shoulders. "Dreven is still at the bar," he says.

"What do you mean." I shake my head. "Why didn't he come back with you two?"

Max speaks up. "They called the cops. He punched a guy."

"He punched a guy?" I shriek. "What the hell? We were all walking out at the same time. How did something escalate to violence in five seconds?"

"I don't know. We were following you three, and the next thing we knew, Dreven's fist was in some guy's face," Max says.

I shake my head. "I can't believe this."

"This isn't a good look, Ms. Stellars." Coach Albright looks at me with a frown. I know his frustration isn't with me but with the situation. Yet I feel as if I've let him down in some way.

"I know. I'll fix it."

Iris steps up behind me. "But the plane's going to leave."

"I'll take a flight out in the morning. I can't just leave one of our players in a Canadian jail." I blow out a breath of annoyance.

Max points toward the exit door. "Try to catch our taxi before he leaves. He was brilliant navigating these streets."

Come to think of it, Jaden and Max left after us due to the punching detour, and they still beat us here. Yes, I definitely want their cab driver.

"I'll come with you," Iris offers.

"No. It's fine. Go home with your husband. There's

no reason for us both to be stuck here." I don't miss the look of relief on her face. Let's face it, who wants to be stuck here? Although a nice hotel room to myself, a hot bath, and a glass of wine isn't a horrible way to spend my birthday eve.

I give Coach a reassuring smile and step out of the plane. My heart sinks when I see the taillights of the SUV disappearing in the snowfall.

"Wait!" I shout, waving my arms, but it's no use. I can no longer see the vehicle, which means he can't see me. I dip my eyes to see Julien's car still sitting beside the plane.

Great.

Jacket wrapped tightly around my waist and my purse in the crook of my arm, I approach the car and open the back door. "Hey, Julien. Any way you can take me back to the bar?"

He looks up from his phone with what can only be described as a grimace. "Um, I'm not taking any more rides today, ma'am. The roads are too bad. Plus, my girlfriend is waiting for me."

"Please?"

"Aren't you leaving? Why do you want to go back?"

"I have to take care of a problem at the bar. They're leaving." I motion toward the plane. "And I'm going to be stuck here if you don't. Please, Julien? I promise to leave you an amazing tip."

"Fine. Get in." He tightens his grasp on the steering wheel.

"Thank you," I say as I slide into the back seat. "You're the best."

I internally take back that last sentiment as soon as he starts driving. His car is fishtailing all over the tarmac. It's only been a couple of minutes since I last left this car, but it feels like the snowfall has tripled in that short amount of time. "Julien, are we going to be able to make it?" I ask, knowing that his answer holds no bearing because regardless of what he says, he's my only option.

"Oh yeah. Piece of cake." He nods as he takes a corner, and the car thumps against something hard, sending me flying in my seat. At least this time, I'm pretty sure it was the curb.

Any annoyance I have toward the weather, Julien's driving ability, or my present situation transforms into anger for Gunner freaking Dreven. After all, this is his fault—all of it.

As Julien drives toward town, the feeling that I'm going to die here in Vancouver, Canada, becomes stronger. I should be flying back to Michigan, where my condo and warm bed await. Instead, I'm practically off-roading through this snowstorm in a vehicle that has no right to be driving in such weather on my way to clean up the mess of an adult hothead. Truthfully, if it wasn't my sole job to keep the team on the good side of the press, I'd let Gunner rot in a Canadian jail cell.

"Just a couple more kilometers, ma'am," Julien calls back, wearing an easy smile that certainly doesn't befit the situation.

His reassurance does little to ease my nerves. The ride back to the bar seems twice as long as the ride to the plane. I press my hands to the back of the seat in front of me in an attempt to keep steady as we bounce and swerve over what I can only hope is the road. I stare at a singular piece of lint on my skirt, focusing on the cream-colored speck in an effort to block out the weather outside. Outside these car windows is nothing but a furious flurry of snow. Raging white snowflakes and a sea of nothingness beyond are all that can be seen. I have no idea how Julien keeps the car on the road, and I've realized falling into a state of total avoidance is my best bet.

Looking out the windows made me feel as if I were trapped inside a violent snow globe being shook by a crazy person. It caused my heart to beat at a level that made me feel as if I were having a heart attack despite knowing it was anxiety. Breathing deeply and focusing on the lint while ignoring the outside world is my survival tactic at this point.

Julien starts shouting, and my body presses against my seat belt, momentum wanting to whip me to the side as the car speeds across the earth in a way I know the driver is not controlling. They say the moment before you die moves in slow motion, and visions of your life flash before your eyes. For me, this isn't entirely true. Time slows, and I'm very aware we're about to crash. Yet no nostalgic visions of my life surface. I expect a few of the good memories I had with my mother to come to mind, but they don't. At the very least, I should be thinking about Tucker—the love of my life—and some of the beautiful times we shared...but nope. Good times in college? Friendships? The taste of a pumpkin spiced latte? Anything?

No.

I'm about to die, and all I can think about is Gunner and how I'm never going to get the chance to tell him how much I hate him. His stupid ass is the reason I'm in this predicament, and I can't even yell at him about it. Not only is he going to be the cause of my death but images of him have stolen the highlight reel of my life that's supposed to play. He can't be my last thought. The summation of my life is so much more than keeping him in line. Isn't it? While rage-inducing, thoughts of Gunner Dreven are also a reminder in my final moments that I failed. I couldn't keep him in check.

A thousand questions and doubts surface. Maybe there is no beautifully touching string of memories because my life wasn't beautiful or touching. It was cold and routine. I tried so hard to be successful and not be anything like my mother, and now, all I have to show for my life is a failed attempt at babysitting a grown-ass man.

My entire body clenches, waiting for impact, and Julien makes a sound resembling a rooster's cock-a-doodle-doo. I'm lifted off my seat, the belt pressing against my thighs before I fall back and hit the side door with a thud.

And then...we're still.

I breathe in deeply, waiting for more. But nothing comes.

Slowly, my muscles unclench, and I open my eyes. Hesitantly, I look out the window. The furious snow globe effect is still in full force, but I'm no longer moving.

"We're alive?" The question leaves my mouth.

Julien laughs. "Of course we're alive. We just slid into a ditch. You're a dramatic one, eh?"

We slid into a ditch? I replay the motions of the last few seconds, and that reality computes. "We're in a ditch?"

"Yeah." Julien scoffs. "We're in a ditch. Slid right off the road. It was to be expected really."

"What?"

"Have you looked out the window, ma'am? These aren't the best driving conditions. Just lucky we made it this far. No worries. We'll just walk the rest of the way."

"I have to walk the rest of the way?" I repeat his statement. "You've got to be kidding me."

"Not at all. It's not that far. In fact, this was a good place to land. My girlfriend's house is a block behind us, and the bar is a couple of blocks in front. Not a problem." Julien zips up his coat and removes his keys from the ignition.

My toes move inside my heels, a reminder that walking through this storm in my current footwear is the definition of a problem.

God, I hate Gunner Dreven.

Pulling out the wad of cash in my wallet, I give it to Julien. I don't have the energy to count it, but regardless of the amount, he's earned it.

He thanks me, and we exit the vehicle. Julien extends his arm and points toward my destination, shouting out directions that I can barely make out above the roar of the wind, and then he's gone.

I secure my purse in the crook of my arm, tighten my much too thin of a jacket, and on unsteady feet, I climb out of the ditch. What was I thinking, wearing high heels and a coat that wouldn't protect me from a bitter wind, let alone the Arctic tundra of snowstorms?

"Oh, I don't know. Maybe I thought I'd be whisked from the plane to the game and back in a nice warm vehicle?" I grumble to myself. "Not on some North Pole version of the TV show *Naked and Afraid*."

While not completely naked, I might as well be with all the warmth my polyester pencil skirt, satin blouse, and thin jacket are holding in. And afraid isn't accurate either—more like furious. I'm in my own personal hell, in a reality show titled *Barely Dressed and Furious in Vancouver*. Admittedly, the title is not as catchy.

I make it out of the ditch and to what I can only assume is the sidewalk. The snow is up to my calves as I trudge in the direction Julien indicated. My teeth chatter, and my toes become more numb with each step until I can't feel them anymore.

Tears roll down my cheeks, freezing on their descent. And while I feel like crying, the tears are less a result of my emotional state and more a side effect of the freezing winds whipping my face and eyes.

I hit a patch of ice beneath the snow and grab a light pole to stop from falling. The bitter wind burns my face as I cling to the frigid pole. Steadying myself, I question my life choices. How did I get here? Do I really care that much about a hockey team to deal with this?

The flicker of the bar sign catches my attention, and my chest swells with renewed confidence. I'm almost there. Twelve or so long strides and I'll be out of this nightmare and into another. But at least that one will have a roof over my head and some heat.

I say a small prayer of thanks when my fingers grasp the handle of the entrance door, and it pulls open, bringing a wave of warmth with it. The journey to this place has tested me to the max, and if I'm honest —it's not been a good look. Some self-reflection is probably in order. But, first, my problem at hand.

The bar has cleared out. The robust party of earlier has been replaced with less than a dozen people scattered about the dimly lit space. It doesn't take longer than a second to find him. Bigger than everyone in this place, he stands out as he leans against the bar top, sipping a beer.

Still unable to feel my toes, I storm toward him with zero professionalism remaining. "You're a fucking asshole."

CHAPTER SIX

GUNNER

My body stiffens at the sound of her voice and the abrasiveness of her words. She and I have never been ones to share pleasantries, but she usually speaks with a certain level of decorum even when she's annoyed as hell. None of that exists now, and I admit, I like it.

"Hey, Princess, you thirsty?" I tip my half-empty bottle of beer toward her.

She halts a foot in front of me and positions her hands on her hips. "Does it look like I'm in the mood for your shit, Gunner?"

I press my lips in a line to stop the grin threatening to appear and the words that I want to say because, honestly, she looks unhinged, like she just wrestled a polar bear. She's covered in snow. Black makeup circles her eyes, and dark streaks stream down over her tomato-red cheeks. Wet locks of her deep red hair fall from her typical updo. She appears to be shaking—from the cold or rage, I'm not sure. But the entire view is something else.

Unable to come up with a response that won't unleash her wrath, I opt to remain quiet. At this moment, if I was betting on Penny or the bear, all my money would be on her. If looks could kill, I'd be dead, for sure.

"Do you know what I went through to get here? Do you realize we're in the midst of the worst storm this area has seen in our lifetime? The team is gone. The plane left. My Uber crashed in a freaking ditch. I had to walk here in three-inch heels!" Her voice shakes with anger. "For you! Because you're too goddamn stupid to keep your hands to yourself."

Anger fills my chest. No one talks to me like that. This is the moment I'd normally fight back. I could put her in her place with a single sentence. Penny and I have had years of arguments, and there have been some memorable ones. I'm not one to feel sorry for the woman. She's not a damsel in distress. She's a force to be reckoned with.

Yet this time feels different.

If Penelope Stellars has an edge of sanity, I think she's there now.

The bartender, a chill as fuck guy named Frank, joins the conversation. "I'm assuming you're the rep from the Cranes?"

"Yes, I'm here on behalf of the Crane Organization." Her tone immediately shifts to the level of professionalism I'm used to when she addresses Frank. "Can you please tell me what happened? And have the cops been called?"

Frank tosses the wet rag in his hand onto the counter behind the bar. "Absolutely, miss. Not sure what was exactly said, but the one over there in the Canucks jersey with that stupid blue wig atop his head said something, and your guy here punched him in the face." He shrugs. "That's all there really was to it. I had to call the officers. I hope you understand. It's our policy. However." He nods toward the front door. "With the storm outside, I doubt they'll be here anytime soon. I'm sure they have a lot more pressing issues than a little bar fight. He's quite hammered." Frank motions toward the guy in the blue wig. "If he's willing to work it out and the two parties come to a resolution that everyone is happy with, I'm fine with everyone going their separate ways. To be honest, I'd like to close up and get home to my family before I'm stuck here."

Penny gives Frank a tight smile. "Thank you. That is what I was hoping." She turns to me and holds out her hand. "Give me your wallet."

"Fuck no." I scowl.

"Now, Dreven."

With a sigh, I pull the leather wallet from my back pocket and place it in her hand. Without another word, she heads over to the table where the douche and his buddies sit.

Penny is in full boss-lady mode as she talks to the guys. I've seen her like this a million times, yet I can't pull my eyes from her. It's fascinating, and a side of her never directed toward me. She stands tall and, despite looking like she was in a bar fight herself with her haphazard appearance, wears a confident elegance that only she could pull off. She moves her hands as she talks and smiles at the piece of shit with the red cheek. To be fair, that was barely a punch. I held back—a lot. If I'd truly been out of control, he wouldn't be sitting there staring at her with a goofy-as-hell grin. He deserved much worse.

She touches his arm with her perfectly manicured nails, and his smile grows. He bobs his head like a child who's just been asked if he wants to go to Disney. Penny laughs, and while it appears completely natural, I know her well enough to see it's all for show.

However, the Canuck buys the charade hook, line, and sinker.

God, I hate him. Just the thought of his existence makes my blood boil. I hate how he's looking at Penny as if he didn't just violate her with his words. What a piece of shit. I want to punch him again, and this time harder. I should, too.

Frank places a glass of ice water in front of me. "Drink this."

"I'm not drunk," I spit out.

"Still. Drink it. You look like you're about to cause more trouble. Your scowl resembles a wolverine gearing up for an attack."

"Does it?" I scoff. "Seen many wolverines preparing to fight, have ya, Frank?"

"Look, big guy. I just want to go home and help my wife prepare for the storm, eh? Let's all play nice."

I turn away from Penny and take a chug of the water. "I'm not going to cause any more problems."

"Good." Frank bobs his chin, picks up the rag, and wipes the bar top.

Taking another sip of water, I throw a glance over my shoulder to see Penny typing something into her phone. The dumbass hockey fan grins at some money in his hand, American bills.

Great.

Releasing a sigh, I turn away and finish the glass of

water. After a moment, Penny walks up beside me and drops my wallet on the counter.

"And?" I scowl.

"Two hundred dollars and box seats at a future Canucks game, one against someone other than us. Let's go."

"Two hundred of my dollars?"

She ignores my question and addresses Frank. "Thanks for your understanding, Frank. We really appreciate it. You and your family stay safe."

"Thank you, miss," he says before furrowing his brows. "Your plane left, eh?"

"Yeah. We'll get a couple of hotel rooms and fly out tomorrow."

Frank presses his lips together and scrunches his nose up before he releases a sigh. "I don't know if either of those will be an option."

"What do you mean?" she asks.

"Well, most of the folks in for the game have already snatched up any available hotel rooms, given the fact that no one's traveling tonight. We also had a couple of musical events in the city today, so I'd say we're at capacity. From what I hear, everything's booked up, and this storm is expected to continue through tomorrow. I'd be surprised if any flights leave tomorrow either."

Penny opens her mouth to speak as all the color

drains from her face. She closes her mouth and stares at Frank. It's rare when this woman doesn't know what to say.

"I doubt that's true. I guarantee there are two rooms up for grabs in this city," I chime in.

Frank shrugs. "I'd call around before you head back out there. Don't want to be caught out in that weather."

Penny and I search for accommodations on our phones. A common goal at hand, we split up the list of hotels in the city and start calling. It's all for not because Frank is correct. The city is full. We've called every establishment, from the one-star motels outside of town up to the five-star places. There is literally nothing.

The wind whips around outside, making an eerie sound while the bar's lights flicker. We're the only ones left in the joint save for Frank, who is kindly staying here for us. Douche boy and his crew headed out somewhere in the midst of our three-star hotel calls. Penny taps her thumb against the bar top and stares off as if in a trance. I can almost hear the wheels turning in her head as she tries to come up with a solution. It's rare that she doesn't have the answer. As annoying as it is, she always does.

I've put us in uncharted territory, a predicament that even little Miss Perfect Penelope Stellars can't talk us out of. An unfamiliar sensation fills my chest, and if I have to guess, I'd say it's something close to remorse.

She turns to me, blinking a few times before stating, "Maybe we can find someone to drive us to another town where we can find a vacancy?"

Frank chimes in. "No one out there is going to drive in this, and even if there were, any place within driving distance would be full. All the sane folk hunkered down hours ago."

"I don't know what to do." There's a quiver in Penny's voice that I haven't heard before, and that uneasy feeling in my chest grows stronger.

Frank releases a sigh. "Well, the wife and I own a small motel a few miles out. It's nothing fancy, and all the normal rooms are booked up. However, we do have a room that we use for storage—you know, boxes of paper towels, toilet paper, and new towels, stuff like that. So besides the floor-to-ceiling boxes, it's just like our other rooms. It's not ideal, but you'll have a place to sleep, and you'll be warm."

Penny stands from the stool. "We'll take it! Oh my gosh, thank you, Frank. You're a lifesaver."

He chuckles. "Don't thank me yet. You haven't seen the place."

"It doesn't matter, I guarantee it's better than sleeping in feet of snow," she says.

"Well, that's true." He grins. "Let me call the wife

and have her change the linens and move the boxes up against the wall to give you a little space. Then we'll head out."

Penny turns toward me. "You better not so much as speak to me all night. If the team wouldn't suffer without you, I'd take the room for myself and leave you out in the cold to freeze."

"You're too kind," I scoff. "Believe me, sleeping in the same room as you isn't high on my list either, Princess."

"Just don't say a word. In fact, it's fine with me if we never speak again."

The odd feeling in my chest from moments ago has been replaced with a very familiar one—disdain. This hot mess of a woman across from me is the bane of my existence, and I have to be stuck in a room with her all night. While I'd never admit it to her, this is all my fault. And I'd be lying if I said I didn't hate myself a little too.

CHAPTER SEVEN

PENELOPE

I have lost count of how many times I thought I was going to die today. The third drive from hell wasn't any less stressful. Different driver, same insanity. While the journey was difficult, I have to give it to Frank. He got us here. Barely. But we're here nonetheless.

He was correct in his description of his motel. It's nothing special. But compared to sleeping out in the cold, it's the flipping Ritz.

We trudge through the calf-high snow. I hold my hand out in front of my face to block the pelts of wetness hitting my skin as Frank leads us to our room. Stopping in front of a door, he hands us two keys, and I thank him again.

"No problem. Have a good night." He nods before hurrying off to no doubt see his family. He's been anxious to get back to them, an endeavor that took longer than it should have because of his willingness to help Gunner and me.

Gunner hasn't said a word since we left the bar, and while it's exactly what I asked him to do, it's annoying at the same time. I don't know what I expect, but I want something. An apology, maybe? That's not his style, so I'm not holding my breath for one. I'm just so angry, and now I have to share a room with the asshole, which makes me even more furious. I want to yell and scream, but that's hard to do with someone who isn't speaking to you. Without his rebuttal, I'm just a crazy person screaming to myself.

With a sigh, I swipe the key card across the reader above the handle, and when the green light flashes, I push the door open. Frank wasn't lying when he said this room was being used for storage. Boxes are stacked to the ceiling along every wall, making a weird paper product fort around the bed. The one bed. My heart drops into my stomach.

"There's only one bed," I cry, looking around the room to make sure I didn't miss the other one. But no —there's probably eight trees worth of boxed toilet paper but not another bed.

Heart beating wildly, I scan the space. It is literally,

a bed, boxes, and a door in the corner that leads to what I assume is the bathroom. That's it. There's no chair or TV or anything to do or anywhere to sit. Sure, it's a step up from dying out in the freezing snow but not a very big one.

Unwelcomed tears fill my eyes as I stand motionless.

A husky voice breaks my trance. "Go take a shower. You're a fucking mess."

His words shock me out of my state. "And you're an ass."

I head to the bathroom anyway because it seems like the only course of action. When my mother came home a drunken mess, I would always put her in the shower. I don't know if there's any solid fact behind it, but it sure feels like a shower makes everything better. Mom always emerged from the shower a little more coherent.

It's been a long, hard day, so a shower can't hurt. Maybe it will even make my current situation seem more tolerable. My stare darts to the singular bed, and I shudder.

Somehow.

It surely can't get any worse.

I flick on the light to the bathroom and close the door behind me, gasping when I catch sight of my reflection. "What in the actual fu..." My voice falters as

I approach the mirror. I look like a rabid half zombie from some post-apocalyptic movie. Seriously, how did Frank, Gunner, or even the blue-wig kid and his friends look at me without laughing?

Note to self: invest in some quality waterproof mascara.

I pull out my hair clip and the parts that were still up fall to meet the rest of the disheveled mess that had worked its way out of the clip at some point during this horrendous night.

Turning on the water, I step in.

The warm water soothes my cool skin, and I welcome it. I already feel myself coming back to life. I wash up with the cheap bar of motel soap. It's not my normal fancy skincare routine, but this face needs a good scrub, discount soap or not.

It's not until I'm out of the shower, a towel wrapped around my hair and another around my body that I realize I have nothing to wear. The last thing I want to do is put that polyester skirt back on.

I open the bathroom door and peek my head out. A T-shirt comes flying toward me, and I grab it before it hits my face.

"You're welcome."

"Why'd you throw me your shirt?"

"Why do you think, Princess? I figured you didn't have anything to wear unless you wear prissy business skirt ensembles in your sleep, too? In that case, I'll take my shirt back." He sits against the headboard, one leg bent and a book in his hand...and he's wearing nothing but boxer shorts.

Quickly, I shut the bathroom door and take a few calming breaths before putting on the T-shirt that smells like him. I slide my panties back on and glance down at my ensemble. Thanks to Gunner's super-tall stature, the T-shirt falls just above my knees.

"Well, it could be worse," I mutter.

Bending at the waist, I flip my head over and scrunch my hair with the towel in an attempt to get as much water from it as possible. When my hair is as dry as it's going to get, I hang up the towel and open the door.

I stand frozen in the doorway as Gunner makes his way toward me. His tall, massive frame is solid muscle, and I can't help but stare as he closes the distance between us. If he wasn't such an asshole, I'd be completely turned on right now. Becoming of his nickname, he is a beast. Every inch of his body is conditioned to perfection. Objectively, his face is quite handsome as well. His dark-black hair lies in spiky chunks, and the scruff on his face is about a week past a five-o'clock shadow. The stubble looks good on him, somehow accentuating his full lips and big brown eyes.

Yeah, if I didn't hate Gunner Dreven with a passion, I could admit that he is sexy as hell.

"Like what you see?" His voice is deep, his question serious.

Furrowing my brows, I focus in on his eyes. "Get over yourself."

He hands me a toothbrush, still in its package, and a mini toothpaste—two items I didn't notice in his hand as I was ogling his body.

I step back as Gunner continues his ascent into the bathroom. "Where did you get these?"

"Frank's wife dropped by while you used up half the water in Vancouver. Frank noticed we had no bags and thought we might need some essentials." He dips his toothpaste-covered toothbrush under the running water before brushing.

"Well, that was nice of her. She didn't have any extra clothes, did she?"

Gunner ignores my question and continues to brush his teeth. It's fine. It's obvious the question was rhetorical. I step beside him and start brushing my teeth. I take in the two of us in the mirror. As a pair, we almost fill up this small bathroom. My hair falls in ringlets over my shoulders, and I don't miss the way Gunner's eyes keep darting toward my reflection in the mirror.

I can't quite read his expression. However, he's never seen me without my hair pulled back and a face full of makeup on. Nor has he ever seen me in anything other than business attire. I'm sure I'm quite unrecognizable.

We finish brushing our teeth in this odd out-of-body experience and retreat to the room of boxes. "How are we going to do this?" I ask.

"What do you mean?"

"The sleeping arrangement. There's only one bed," I snap, gesturing to the bed before us. Not that the gesture was necessary, given it's the only space in the room not filled with junk save for the walkway to the door and to the bathroom.

"Well, unless you're a fan of sleeping atop boxes or can find a clean spot on the floor, there really aren't many options."

"You're not sleeping with me," I protest, and a whine that makes me cringe accompanies my words. *Pull yourself together, Penny.*

He releases a raspy chuckle. "I think we both know that's not true."

"What does that mean?"

"What do you think it means?" He stares down at me, his facial features unmoving.

A shiver runs down my spine, and I feel a mixture of annoyance and something else that I can't quite put my finger on. "This is the worst day ever." I sigh.

"It's really that bad?" Gunner quirks a brow, and I

want to slap it right off him. I feel his judgment radiating from him.

"Of course it is!" I thread my fingers through my hair and release a pent-up groan. "This has been the worst day. I shouldn't be here. In fact, I'm sick of this stupid job. I'm the public relations manager for one of the best hockey teams in the nation, yet my entire job consists of babysitting you! A grown man who can't keep his hands to himself! And now, we're stuck here in this shithole for God knows how long with nothing but the items in my purse. My only choice is to sleep half-naked with a man I despise or on the floor atop carpet that probably has enough germs to start a plague. My birthday is tomorrow, and all I wanted to do was spend it at home, comfortable, in my own bed watching *Friends*!" An errant tear streams down my face, and I swipe the back of my hand across my cheek.

He narrows his gaze. "Don't forget that we share a birthday, Princess, and not that I care—it's just another day to me—but I would also rather be anywhere other than here."

"Well, you have no one to blame but yourself for that one," I say with a roll of my eyes.

He reaches out and pulls on the end of a lock of my hair, the movement oddly personal, especially coming from him. "You should wear your hair down more."

"You should keep your opinions to yourself." I glare up at him.

"You don't need to wear all that makeup either."

I take a step back, my eyes bulging. "And you don't need to tell me what to do. What's going on here? On a normal day, you communicate in grunts and scowls, and now you're giving me advice on my appearance?"

He shakes his head, frowning. "You know, you don't always have to be a bitch."

My mouth falls open. "Yes, I do! Because you're always an ass!"

Turning away from me, he gets into bed. "Get the light."

My arms cross, and I take my defensive stance, ready to fight. Gunner and I have been in more than enough verbal sparring matches. Only after his order about the light, he says nothing else. His back is turned to me, and I have to question the insane desire within me to keep our argument going. He's retreated and moved on, yet here I stand, ready for another round.

Maybe I am the problem?

No, it's definitely him.

I wait for a few beats, weighing my options, and I come up short. There really is only one option.

Ugh.

After I switch off the light, I climb into bed, facing away from Gunner. I'm very aware of his back against mine, but I do everything in my power to ignore it. The room is silent save for our breaths and the violent screeches of the wind outside. This is quite a storm. I guess, being in any bed, even one with Gunner, is better than being out there.

We lay in silence for what seems like forever. Despite the exhaustion that covers me, I can't sleep. I need to turn to my other side, but facing him isn't an option.

I have a pinched disc in my lower back from falling an entire story and landing on the corner of hard wooden steps on my tailbone. I was eight years old when I had been leaning against the railing in the attic when it broke, causing me to fall onto the steps below. It was so painful at the time. I remember lying in bed for weeks because it hurt too much to move. I eventually healed, but I couldn't run for almost a year. Now, it really doesn't bother me unless I'm lifting a lot of heavy items or sleeping in the same position for too long. At home, I wake up multiple times a night to switch positions, which is not something I can do here. The two of us take up an entire bed. Not only do I have to share a bed with my enemy but it has to be a double at that. A king-sized bed would've been too much to ask for on this day of hell.

"Happy birthday," Gunner whispers, and it startles me. I thought he was asleep.

Giving in, I turn to face him, and the stretch of my lower back gives me a sigh of relief. "What?" I say quietly.

Gunner turns to face me. There's just enough ambient lighting in the dark space for me to make out his features. "It's midnight here, so happy birthday. I mean, it was our birthday three hours ago in Michigan but just now, here."

"You're so strange here," I say in response.

He looks at me in question.

"I'm just saying, you're different. Nicer, even."

He releases a breath. "I just don't think constantly fighting when we're stuck here together is the best course of action."

"It does make our situation that much more miserable."

"Exactly."

I bite my lip. "So in Vancouver, we can be on a break from us."

"Meaning?"

"Well, while we're stuck here, we can be different people. We can pretend to enjoy one another's company. We can use kind words—"

He cuts me off. "You're going to use kind words? Toward me?"

My snappy retort is on the tip of my tongue. Put it off to fatigue or birthday nostalgia or the simple fact that I'm in bed with Gunner in a glorified storage closet, but I bury the rude response and instead say, "Yes because while we're here, you're not the asshole I despise, and I'm not the bitch you hate. We're just two people. Friends even."

"It would make everything a little more bearable."

"Right? I'm just so stressed and tired and simply don't have the energy to hate you right now."

He gives me another half chuckle, the second one of the evening and probably the second one I've ever heard leave his lips. "Whatever makes it easier on you, Penny."

My lip tilts up. "You called me by my name."

"That's what fake friends do. Fake friends also give advice, and I wanted to give you some, starting with my number-one stress reliever...well, I guess number two because I'd say number one is a good workout, especially one on the ice."

Gunner's face, barely visible in the dim light, is mere inches from my own. I'm taken aback by how much he's talking to me. It's mildly unsettling, really. "What's your number two stress-relieving advice?" I ask hesitantly.

"Sex."

I push my hand against his chest in an effort to create some distance between us. He grabs my wrist and holds my palm against his bare skin. "What are you doing?" I whisper-shriek.

"I want you to feel how fast my heart is beating, being in this bed so close to you. I'd venture a guess that your heart is beating just as fast."

"No, it's not," I lie. Holy heck, the skin on my palm is on fire from this simple touch.

"Tell me you're not curious." His grasp on my hand remains firm.

"I'm not at all."

He shakes his head. "You're lying."

"Gunner, we can't. That would open up a whole can of worms that neither of us wants to deal with."

"Why? You said it yourself. We're different people here. You've had a one-night stand before, yes?"

"Yeah."

"So you enjoyed yourself with someone for one night and then left it at that. Right?"

I sigh. "Yeah, but that's different. You and I work together. It might create issues."

"Issues how? You'll hate me again? That's going to happen anyway. We'll go back to Michigan tomorrow, and this will all be a distant memory. You can forget all about your worst day ever. But until then, we might as well make our time here a little more fun." With one hand still holding my wrist, he lifts the other and holds it inches from my chest. "I'll tell you what. If your heart isn't racing as much as mine is, we'll let it go. But if it is, we'll continue this discussion. Can I touch your chest?"

Before I can stop my traitorous head, it nods in permission.

I suck in a breath when Gunner dips his hand under the bottom of my shirt. He doesn't touch me as he moves his hand up my body, but the heat warms my skin all the same. His palm moves over my bare breasts, and my nipples harden, wanting to feel his touch, but he doesn't linger. His palm presses against the skin of my chest, where my heart beats violently.

"I knew you were lying." His words, all husky and needy, are barely a whisper.

"I'm not," I lie again. My stubbornness fights against the inevitable. I close my eyes and revel in the sensation of his palm against my chest.

"No?"

My tongue peeks out to wet my lips as my head shakes.

"If you say so." He leans in and says against my neck, "There is another way to figure this out. Do I have your permission?"

He doesn't even have to say what for because I already know. "Yes," I pant, my chest rising and falling in labored breaths.

His hand leaves my chest and skims down my

body, this time touching me on its descent. Eyes still closed, I feel every inch of it down to my core. His touch is like fire, and my body is begging for the burn. The urge to explode in a fiery rage of pleasure pounds through every inch of me, and we've barely started. He slides his hand into my underwear, and I bite my lip, my body clenching as I wait for his touch.

He slips a finger into my wet opening. "Fuuuck me," he groans into my neck. "You're fucking soaked. You want me as much as I want you. Admit it."

"I don't," I whine as his finger starts to move inside me. "Ahhh…" I moan as he rubs against my front wall. He inserts a second finger and pulls them out, sliding my wetness over my bundle of nerves. His two fingers enter me again as his thumb circles my clit. "Oh my God," I pant, my hips moving to meet his thrusts. He works me until my whole body hums on the verge of release. "Tell me you want me, Penny. Say the words."

"No."

I feel the crescendo forming inside me, and I'm so ready to explode. He moves his fingers as the sensations build. I'm panting, feeling everything he's giving me. I don't know if I've ever enjoyed someone's fingers this much. "Oh," I cry out. I'm seconds from release.

And then it stops.

He pulls his fingers away, and it's a splash of cold water to my libido. "What are you doing?" I gasp.

"You said you don't want me."

Oh, this prick.

"Gunner," I plead, needing the release.

"No," he states, his voice firm.

"Fine! I fucking want you, Gunner Dreven. Scratch that, I fucking need you. Now, get down there and finish what you started!"

A smile crosses his face, and I have to admit, it's a beautiful sight.

He pulls the blankets off us and moves down between my legs. He shimmies my panties down my legs and discards them on the side of the bed. Placing his hands on my knees, he spreads me open wide. "Much better." His fingers slide back into me, and I cry out. Only this time, it's his tongue that moves against the most sensitive spot. Oh, and what a glorious tongue it is.

"Yes!" I scream into the lust-filled air. I can't even comprehend what's happening and with who because I'm so overcome with pleasure. Every hair on my body stands at attention as a wave of goose bumps covers my skin. Gunner continues to work magic with his mouth and fingers, and it's only a matter of seconds before I'm crying out as my orgasm hits hard. He continues to lick me as I ride the waves of release.

When I'm finished, he kisses up my body, removing

his shirt from me in the process, pulling it over my head and tossing it to the floor.

His mouth finds mine, and I kiss him hard, threading my fingers through his hair as our tongues move against one another. He gently bites my bottom lip and pulls his mouth away before he gets off the bed. I prop myself up on my elbows and watch him in confusion as he maneuvers toward the windows, opening the blackout curtains.

The room is illuminated with light from the moon bouncing off the white snow. Suddenly aware that I'm very naked, I pull the sheet over my body.

"What are you doing?" Gunner asks. "I want to see you."

"Why don't we keep it under the sheet," I say. I'm aware that Gunner can pick up almost any woman at any given bar on most nights of the week. I've seen him leave with women who could be supermodels. While I feel I've accepted my full-figured body for the most part, there's some buried insecurity there. In comparison, I carry more weight than the women Gunner normally sleeps with, and despite just having his face between my legs, I feel very vulnerable.

Gunner shakes his head and closes the gap between us. He rips the sheet off the bed. "Stand up," he orders.

It's unlike me to follow commands, but I find myself doing just that.

As I stand bare in front of Gunner, his heated stare moves from my face to my feet and back again. "You are fucking beautiful." He presses his hands flat against my chest, running them over my shoulders, down my collarbone, and to my breasts. He holds one in each of his hands. Mouth slightly agape, he breathes heavy. He flicks my nipples with his thumbs before continuing his descent over my stomach and hips. He takes my ass in his hands and squeezes. "Your body is a fucking dream, Penny. It's curvy, and soft, and so fucking sexy. You don't even know how many times I've stared at you in your tight business suits, wanting to know what you looked like beneath it all. I need you to believe me when I tell you that you look better than I could've imagined."

I nod hesitantly.

"Pull down my boxers," he says, and I do as instructed. His massive length stands at attention. "Do you see what your body does to me?" His voice is gravelly and heavy with lust.

I nod.

"Do you see how much I want you?"

I nod again.

"You are a lot of things, Penelope Stellars, and sexy as fuck is one of them. Do you hear me?"

"Yes," I say.

"Good. Now suck."

I should argue and tell him that he's not my boss and doesn't have the right to order me around like that, but I don't say anything. I can't because his hardness is in my mouth in a matter of seconds. Not because he told me to, but because I want it there. Desperately.

I want to taste him the way he tasted me. I want to please him the way he pleased me. I want to bring him to the brink of insanity and watch him fall over into pleasure. I want him more than I've ever wanted anyone, and I'm too insane with lust to stop and figure out what all this means.

Circling my hand around the base of his shaft, I pump my hand back and forth as my mouth takes him in as far as I can. I swirl my tongue around his tip and move it up and down over him. His head falls back, and he threads his fingers through my hair as he groans toward the ceiling. He pumps himself into my mouth as he pulls my head against him. I take him in until he's hitting the back of my throat. I'm out of control with the need to taste him and watch him lose control. He's so close. I press my knees together, trying to squash the pounding of desire between my legs. Seeing Gunner chase ecstasy and knowing I'm the one who's giving it to him is the strongest aphrodisiac I've experienced.

Just when I think he's going to fall into oblivion, he pulls away. "Condom," he states.

"My purse," I gasp between breaths.

He retrieves a condom from my purse and slides it over his length while he eyes me with a heated stare. "I don't know how to take you," he utters. "I want you in so many ways." After a beat, he pushes me onto the bed so I'm facing him. He hooks one of his arms under my knee, lifting that leg back and opening me wide for him. "I want to see your face when we come."

With that, he slides inside me, filling me up completely, and starts to move. Each movement sends a jolt of electricity through my body. I claw at his arms, wanting more.

"You want it harder?" His voice is strained. "I don't want to hurt you."

"I can take all of you. I want to feel all of you."

He growls. "Fucking-A, Stellars. You're going to kill me with that mouth of yours."

He picks up the pace. His thrusts become more forceful as he slams into me, harder and harder. We both moan as he enters me over and over. It's the most amazing feeling, and I don't want it to stop. I've had my share of sex, but this, right here, is on a whole other level. It's too good. Our bodies fit perfectly as he moves exactly how I need him to.

"I'm going to come," I cry out, feeling the warmth of release fill every pore of my body.

"Open your eyes," he orders, the words almost pained as he builds toward his own release. "I want to see your eyes as you come."

My orgasm hits hard, and I hold Gunner's stare as I scream. He crashes over into oblivion with me, his mouth falling open as he vocalizes his pleasure, never taking his eyes off me. He pulls out of me and discards the condom before plopping onto the bed beside me. The two of us lie naked next to one another, staring at the ceiling as we catch our breath.

"Happy birthday to me," Gunner says, causing me to chuckle. "That was some amazing sex."

"I don't feel so stressed anymore," I quip.

"See, I told you."

I don't recognize the man beside me. This is a side of him I've never seen in more ways than one. "Who knew you had a personality? I never knew you were more than a goal-tending, grunting beast."

"That's my gift to you," he teases. "Just know, this version of me expires the second we leave this room."

"Oh, I have no doubts about that."

We situate ourselves on our pillows, pulling the blankets up over our naked bodies. Gunner wraps an arm around me, and I lean against his chest. Our legs intertwine with one another. I'm sated, exhausted, and a little confused, so sleep pulls me under quickly.

And it's the best night of sleep I've had in a long time.

CHAPTER EIGHT

GUNNER

It takes me a moment to remember where I am, but the musty smell of cardboard and the howl of the wind outside brings the memories of yesterday back in full clarity.

I stretch my arms out over my head, my joints cracking with the motion. Man, I slept like a rock. Yesterday was a long-ass day with the game and the hard loss, the bar, the fight—if we can even call it that —the storm, and the sex. Oh, the sex. Speaking of...

Opening my eyes, I prop myself up on my elbows and look around the room. The bathroom door is open, and the lights are off. Unless Penny has crawled into one of these boxes of toilet paper, it's safe to say she's not here. Where she'd be, I have no idea. Snow drifts cover the window, allowing only a few-inch gap at the top to see that the white flakes are still falling. I sure hope they've cleared the runways so we can get out of here and back home.

Retrieving my discarded boxers from the floor, I put them on before heading to the bathroom. After I brush my teeth, I return to the bed and check my phone. I have a few texts from the guys, but nothing from Penny indicating where she may be.

The fact is, she may be long gone. I wouldn't be surprised if I pushed her too far last night. While she wanted it in the moment, the light of a new day could be bringing major regrets.

With that thought, the door opens, and Penny enters. She's wearing my T-shirt with her pencil skirt and her thin-ass jacket over the pair...and of course, her tall heels—the perfect footwear for any record-breaking snowstorm. Her red hair falls down her back and over her shoulders in big, bold ringlets. The look is mesmerizing and hot as fuck. That wild, curly hair does something to me. Her face is still makeup-free, and I was serious last night when I said she didn't need all that stuff on her face if she didn't want it. Her natural beauty is unique and captivating.

I'm so focused on her appearance and what it's doing to me that I don't notice the plate in her hand until she's standing before me with a wide smile. A grinning Penny is a little off-putting, another facet of her that I've never seen. She's always so serious at work, and she's especially somber with me.

"You're up." There she goes with that smiling thing again. "I thought I'd venture out to see if I could find us some breakfast. First, let me just say that we're not going anywhere. Everything is shut down. They're expecting a bunch more snow today on top of the insane snowfall yesterday. I had a cup of coffee with Frank's wife, Alice. She's so nice. But all she had to offer was yesterday's uneaten donuts. So..." She lowers the plate to my eye level. "Happy birthday."

The plate holds four donuts with different brightly colored frosting and sprinkles on each one. I swear my heart stops beating as a lump of emotion fills my throat. I haven't eaten a frosted donut with sprinkles since the last birthday I celebrated with my mother during my senior year of high school. She didn't make it to my nineteenth birthday, freshman year of college, because she was dead by then.

"You don't like donuts?" she asks.

I force down all of my emotions. I may have fucked Penny, but we're not friends. I'm not going to share my deepest regret with her, nor am I going to let her see my pain—the ever-present heartache I feel whenever something reminds me of my mother.

Clearing my throat, I say, "No, they're fine."

"It's not a birthday cake or anything, but they're festive and really...our only option." She sets the plate on the bed and kicks off her heels before removing her jacket and skirt. "God, that skirt is uncomfortable." She sits across from me on the bed, the plate of donuts between us.

"Should we make a wish?"

"We did that at the party last week. I think we're good."

She shrugs. "True, but it wasn't our real birthday, you know? Seriously, let's just do it. Close your eyes and make a wish."

I do as instructed because I can't come up with a good reason not to. When I've spoken my wish in my head, I open my eyes.

"Done?" she asks.

"Done."

"Okay, you get the first pick of the stale donuts," she offers.

I pick up the one with pink frosting and multicolored sprinkles because it looks just like the last one my mother got me. I take a bite, and a wave of nostalgia hits me. All the little things my mother did for me in the moments of quiet because she wasn't able to love me out loud come back. She would give me secret looks and smiles, a squeeze of the hand, a whisper of praise, and an early morning birthday donut. In her weakness and inability to protect or stand up for herself, she kept me as safe as possible by keeping me invisible. She allowed herself to remain the target so I wouldn't be. And because I couldn't save her, she's gone.

In all its sweetness, this donut reminds me of the good, but it also brings memories of the bad crashing down, and there was so much bad.

She chews her donut. "Oh my gosh, these are awful. So stale."

"They're stale?" I ask.

"Horribly stale."

At this moment, I realize all the donuts I've eaten in my life have been stale because this is exactly what they've tasted like. It makes sense. I'm guessing my mom got them a day or two before my birthday, whenever she could get away unnoticed. She could've even bought day-old discount ones at the bakery. Money was always tight. As I've only ever eaten donuts with my mother, it never dawned on me that I was eating stale ones.

I take another bite of the donut while closing off my traitorous emotions. A self-induced pity party isn't something I condone.

Penny continues, "But I'm not sure if we'll eat anything else today, so they'll have to do."

"It's really that bad out there?" I take another bite of the donut.

"According to Alice, yeah. It might take a couple of days to dig everyone out and clear the roads, especially with the snow still coming down. I mean, I really hope it's not as bad as they say, but I guess we'll see."

My thoughts immediately go to our game schedule. "We play Tampa Bay in three days. We better be back by then."

"Let's hope so."

The conversation is pleasant, and it's clear we're still on that break we discussed last night, which is good. Consecutive days in this small space with someone you despise would be awful. However, a friend—especially one with benefits—is manageable.

"Did you have any birthday traditions growing up?" Penny asks, and my whole body stiffens.

"No. Birthdays were never a big deal." I opt to keep things simple. "You?"

"No, and for the same reason."

It's obvious there is more to her story, just as there is more to mine. It's also clear that neither of us wants to talk about it. Instead, we chat about the team and our performance this season. It's neutral territory, one in which we share a mutual investment. It's a safe topic that will keep our faux friendship thriving and fills the silence.

After breakfast, I follow Penny on the path between the boxes to the bathroom, where we brush our teeth.

This entire situation is surreal. Never in a million years did I imagine I'd be standing in some motel bathroom in Canada beside Penelope Stellars, let alone having some of the best sex of my life with her.

Memories of last night play in my mind like some fantasy porn reel tailored just for me. Because let's face it, Penny—in body—is my ideal woman. Her curves, wild, fiery curls, pale skin, and doe eyes drive me crazy.

I stare at her reflection in the mirror, thinking of her now and then, and my pulse quickens. It's probably a good thing that she doesn't wear her hair down at work. It'd be impossible to hate her the way I do because she makes me wild with longing.

Penny spits and rinses out her mouth with water. I follow suit.

"What are you thinking?" she asks, raising a brow.

I shake my head, huffing out, "Nothing."

Her gaze leaves my face, dropping to the obvious bulge in my boxer shorts. "Nothing?"

My body betrays me. It's clear I want her, and she knows it. Cautious isn't a word that is normally used to describe me, but our situation hangs on a small precipice of joviality. Everything is cool between us, and we need to keep it that way since we're stuck here.

We've avoided all mention of last night's adventures, but the reasons for why are unclear. For all I know, she could regret it, and if that's the case, the last thing I want to do is make her uncomfortable.

This isn't my normal. If a woman wants me, I know it. With Penny, it's just not black and white. Our current cohabitation brings a whole shit ton of gray.

"Nothing?" she repeats. "Interesting. Well, I'm definitely thinking something." She crosses her arms in front of her, grabbing the hem of my shirt and lifting it over her head, leaving her standing in just her panties.

I swallow hard, the intensity of my need growing.

She shimmies off her panties and stands before me completely naked. I'm not shy about scanning her body. I want to see every inch. She was beautiful in the moonlight, but this view is even better. She's the opposite of last night when she wanted to cover up. Pride fills my chest, knowing she's no longer ashamed of her curves with me, and I aided her with the newfound confidence. She has the most gorgeous set of tits I've seen—big, natural, and pale with a smattering of tiny freckles. My mouth waters, imagining sucking on her taut nipple. Raising my hands, I reach out to touch her breasts, but before I make contact, she takes a step back.

I lift my gaze, and she wears a smirk. "I believe I recall you making me say what I wanted out loud last night. In fact, I remember screaming it, so I believe a little reciprocation is in order. I need to hear the words. Everything you're thinking, I want to know."

"You know," I say, my voice low.

She shakes her head. "I want you to say it."

I advance, stepping toward her until her back is against the wall. I lift her chin with a finger, and our brown stares lock. "I think you are the sexiest woman I've ever met. Everything about you drives me crazy. Right now, I want to bury myself so deep inside you that all you can do is scream my name. Is that clear enough for you?"

Her lips part, and her chest rises and falls as she breathes heavy. "Yeah. That's good." Her voice is weighted with need. Leaning in, I press my mouth to hers. She welcomes my tongue in with a sigh. The kiss is raw and deep, and utterly tantalizing.

When I pull away, she whispers, "Shower first?"

My heart races, and I'm feeling drunk with longing. I nod, and reaching past her, I turn on the shower. I remove my boxer shorts, and when the water is warm, we step in.

The hot water sprays across my back as we kiss. After a few minutes of perfect kisses, she lathers up some soap and massages my skin. Her touch feels so good, and I close my eyes to really experience every moment.

Unable to wait any longer, I reach between her thighs. Her breath leaves her mouth in a moan as I insert two fingers inside her. I begin what I hope is a tantalizing rhythm, and based on her vocalizations, I'd say it is. She splays her hand against the shower wall to steady her quivering body. I kneel in front of her and pull one of her legs over my shoulder. Without slowing my pulsating fingers, my tongue begins a cadence of its own, flicking against the spot that needs it the most. She whimpers from the sweet, torturous sensations and throws her head back, facing the shower ceiling, moaning loudly.

"Omigod, omigod, Gunner," she chants, her body meeting my movements.

As my tongue works, my fingers rub against her G-spot, and her moans grow louder. Her inner walls begin to pulse around my fingers as her hips rock to counter the motion of my mouth. She's so close. She lifts one of her hands off the shower wall and threads it through my wet hair, pushing my head against her core. I consume her with everything I have, hungry for her release to wreck her body.

"I'm so close. Don't stop. Don't stop," she begs in desperation.

And then she's falling into ecstasy. She holds my head against her core as her body starts trembling. I feel the evidence of her release around my fingers as she continues to moan into the steam of the shower. When she starts to come down from her high, I remove my fingers and stand.

Her eyes are hooded, drunk with lust, and she's so irresistible. Grabbing the soap, I move to wash her, but before I do, she drops to her knees.

I inhale sharply when she grabs my length and works it in her slick hands from the tip to the base, over and over again.

Holding me at the base, she covers me with her mouth, working her tongue in circles around the tip. She begins a delicious rhythm, greedily taking me in her mouth with moans of pleasure. She removes her hand from my base and grabs the back of my thighs, pulling me as far into her throat as she can take, still working her tongue around me.

"Oh, fuck…"

The sensation is too good.

The fire building at my core erupts and sends a deep, raw, mind-blowing burn through my body, out to my fingertips, down to my toes, up to my scalp, and everywhere in between, scalding me with fierce pleasure. At the peak of my sensation, my hand grabs her head as I empty inside her mouth, and she takes it all. I groan loudly as waves of pleasure shake my body.

I moan as Penny slowly removes her mouth, licking along my length as she does. She swirls her tongue around the tip, and the visual alone almost makes me want to come again. I fall to my knees to meet her, and my lips attach to hers. Our tongues tangle, and I kiss her hard as the water falls around us, streaming down my face and over our lips as I consume her.

I break our kiss. "Let's finish washing up and move this to the bed."

She splays her hands across my chest. "And why is that, Gunner?"

I like this playful side of Penny. Who knew that all that was needed to break her free of her icy exterior was a solid orgasm? "Because I want to fuck you. Again, and again, and again. I want your body to be so wrecked with pleasure that you can't stand straight. I want to fuck you until we pass out from exhaustion, and then I want to wake up and do it again. How does that sound?"

Her tongue peeks out, and she licks her lips as her pupils dilate. "I like that plan."

The truth is, at this moment, I don't care about our game against Tampa Bay in three days. I hope we're snowed in for a good while because I know nothing will be the same when we leave this storage closet of a motel room. Once we check out, I'll never see this side of Penny again. I'll never feel her come around me or hear her moans of pleasure. I'll forever be chasing sex with this level of chemistry. I will once again be her annoyance, and she'll once again be a moody witch.

No, something about this place and these circumstances have transported us to this twilight world where things are different. And I want to savor this time with Penny while I can.

CHAPTER NINE

PENELOPE

Gunner's arm drapes over my bare waist as his chest rises and falls in slumber. True to his word, we had some hot sex until we crashed with exhaustion. The man isn't just a beast on the ice, and it doesn't surprise me one bit. Someone who is as intense and broody as him is bound to be good in the sex department.

I never thought I'd spend the entirety of my birthday with Gunner Dreven inside me. But I have to say, as far as birthdays go, it was one of the more enjoyable ones, if not the most fun. This is all still so weird, but I've decided to cope by just not thinking about it. Compartmentalization at its finest. I know two Gunners—the asshole of the Cranes hockey team and the other one who only resides in Canada and I refer to as the orgasm king. It's a little much but completely accurate. The guy is a master at knowing his way around my body.

Trying not to wake him, I reach for my phone on the nightstand. It's nine o'clock in the morning, and all we've consumed in a twenty-four-hour period is two stale donuts each. However, we've exerted thousands of calories, and my body definitely needs some nourishment. My stomach aches, and I feel weak. The only way to continue enjoying the orgasm king is with some fuel in the form of calories. Maybe they have a vending machine nearby?

I move Gunner's arm off me and start to sneak out of the bed. His grasp catches my arm before I succeed. "Where are you going?"

"I was going to look around this place for something to eat."

"No. Stay. I need you. See, I'm using my words." His voice is still heavy with slumber, and it's mildly adorable. Admittedly, orgasm king is pretty damn sexy.

"You want a repeat of yesterday?" I ask.

"That is my plan, yes."

"Well, I don't know about you, but if I don't get some nourishment, I won't have the energy for that." Gunner's stomach rumbles as I finish my sentence, causing me to chuckle. "And you won't either. Come on. Get up. You can go search for food with me."

"Well, I'm going to need my shirt back for that." He sits up, stretching his arms over his head as his back cracks.

I sigh and retrieve his shirt from the floor before tossing it to him. "Yeah, I figured. Which means I have to put my suit back on." The thought of putting on my uncomfortable outfit yet again is depressing. Canada Penny is different too. She walks around naked without makeup and wears her lion's mane of curls down. She's lighter and even a little cheeky. I don't recognize her, but I like her. The fact is, I'm going to miss her.

Yet Canada Penny wouldn't fly in Michigan. I've spent years designing the life I wanted, being strong, being the opposite of my mother, building walls, and protecting myself. If I'm being honest, Canada Penny reminds me of my mother without the drinking, and that is scary. She's cool here in the make-believe bubble that Gunner and I are in, but she'd never make it at home. Mainly because I wouldn't allow it.

Once we're dressed and ready, we head out. As is with motels, each door exists to the outside. There is no interior hallway. So I have to trudge through knee-high snow drifts in my bare legs and three-inch heels, a quite difficult feat.

I yelp when Gunner grabs my waist from behind, flips me around, and throws me over his shoulder. "What are you doing?" I yell. "Put me down."

"And watch you struggle to walk in that ridiculous outfit? No."

Ass toward the sky, I stay strung over Gunner's shoulder as we move toward the motel's office. A bell chimes when he pushes the glass door open. He sets me down on the worn red carpet.

"You two surviving?" a familiar voice asks.

I turn to see Frank and Alice. "We're trying," I say. "Good morning. The bars not open today?"

Frank chuckles. "I couldn't make it there if I tried. Roads aren't fit for driving just yet, especially not out this way."

I'm very aware of Gunner's presence behind me. He doesn't say anything, though, and lets me do the talking. "So there probably aren't any restaurants open nearby?"

"No, there are not," Alice says.

"Vending machines?" I say with hope in my voice.

"That was picked dry yesterday." Frank looks back and forth between Gunner and me.

I look back at Gunner with a frown. It's one thing to be stranded, but starving is another.

Alice waves us forward. "Don't you fret, sweetie. We won't let you go hungry. Follow me."

"You have a kitchen here?" I ask as Gunner and I follow her around the check-in counter and through the door behind it.

"Yeah, in our home," she says with a laugh.

It never dawned on me that they live here, but I guess it should have. Sure enough, beyond the office is an entire living space. We follow Alice through the living room and closed doors, which I assume lead to the bedrooms. A round of screams comes from one of the rooms, and I look at the closed door, startled.

"Don't mind them." Alice waves her hand. "Boys and their video games. It can get pretty intense. Our three have joined forces to fight," she calls over her shoulder, "what is it, honey?"

Frank answers. "Aliens. They're battling aliens. It's a new multiplayer game they got for Christmas, and they've been obsessed with it since. So much so they get up early on a snow day just to play. I know we shouldn't let them play video games for hours, but to be honest, it's something they can all do together."

"And get along while doing it!" Alice adds. "We asked them to play a game of Scrabble yesterday, but they weren't having any of that." She opens the refrigerator and starts pulling out ingredients. "How does pancakes, bacon, and eggs sound? I'm guessing the only thing you ate yesterday were those donuts?"

Gunner speaks up. "That all sounds great. Thank you."

"Oh, sweetie." Alice eyes me up and down. "You've been in that outfit and those heels for three days. We'd be happy to give you some more comfortable clothes."

I shake my head. "That's not necessary. I'm fine, really."

Alice is half my size, and Frank is an average-sized man. Unlike Frank, I have hips and curves. There's no way I'd fit in either of their clothes, and it would just be embarrassing to inform them of that. I carry my weight well and know what clothing items flatter my figure, so much so that I think people think I'm smaller than I am.

Back in college, I was talking to this boy who worked for a popular clothing store. To be nice, he used his discount to buy me a dress—a very non-stretchy dress in a size six. I was a size twelve, then. When I told him the dress was too small, he looked at me confused and asked if I was serious. He literally couldn't believe the dress didn't fit. What I didn't tell him was that it was multiple sizes too small. I thanked him for the gesture but had him take it back. I still think about that embarrassment and avoid any situations that would put me in that place again. Maybe it's part of the reason I don't have any close girlfriends and never take Iris up on her offer to go shopping. The last thing I want to have to say is, "Sorry, this store doesn't carry my size," because most boutiques don't carry a size eighteen. Most days, my size doesn't faze me because I know I look good. Trying on clothes that might be too small is, however, a fear that I don't want to face.

"You should change. You were just saying how uncomfortable you are," Gunner murmurs—his words only intended for me.

"I'm fine!" I snap, a little too aggressively. "I'm sorry. I just don't want to change. Okay?"

He raises his hand in mock surrender and steps away from me.

Alice busies herself in the kitchen while Gunner, Frank, and I sit at the bar top that looks into the kitchen. "So I hear that you two are stuck here because Mr. Hockey Player punched someone," she questions with a chuckle.

Gunner quirks a brow and turns to Frank. "Isn't there some sort of bartender-client confidentiality you're supposed to abide by?"

Alice cuts in before Frank can answer. "Oh, sweetie. This guy tells me everything. Every. Little. Thing. Honestly, it's one of the perks of owning a bar—the best stories. The two of us never run out of things, or should I say people, to talk about."

Frank holds out his hand toward his wife, palm up.

"Let me reintroduce you to my wife, the town gossip." He grins.

"He deserved it." Gunner finally huffs out in reply.

I never did ask him why he hit the guy. I didn't care at the time since I was just so mad. "Why did you hit him?"

He gives me a subtle shake of his head. "It's not important."

Alice flips a pancake on the griddle. "Well, I'm just glad we could help you out. I know it's not the best accommodations, but at least it's warm."

"We were very lucky to be at Frank's bar," I state. "And the room is great. Beats the alternative, that's for sure."

"Isn't that the truth?" She retrieves the syrup and butter from the fridge and places them on the bar before us.

A few moments later, a delicious-smelling breakfast is set before us, complete with fluffy pancakes, crispy bacon, and the most delicious scrambled eggs I've ever tasted. It's hard to tell whether they really are better than any eggs I've had in my lifetime or if I'm just that hungry. I give a half-assed attempt at eating with a little bit of decorum before I just start shoveling food into my mouth. I feel as if I haven't eaten in days...and, well...that's pretty much true.

Alice raises a brow as I shove a forkful of eggs into

my mouth. "The secret ingredient is heavy whipping cream. I whipped some eggs up with the cream when I started on my keto diet, and I've vowed it's the only way I'll make them from now on."

Gunner takes a swig of orange juice. "Everything is wonderful. Thank you. Please let me know how much we owe you."

Alice smiles as she places a plate into the dishwasher. "You don't owe us a thing for this meal, sweetie. Consider us even for charging you to stay in what can only be described as our storage closet." She chuckles.

Frank joins his wife in the kitchen, and the two work in tandem to clean up. I don't miss their subtle touches and loving smiles toward one another; it's sweet.

"How long have you two been together?" I ask.

"Basically our whole lives," Alice says with a laugh. "Frank was my neighbor growing up, so we've known each other since the beginning, but we became official when we were fifteen and were married the week after I turned eighteen. My parents weren't thrilled that we ran off and got married before we'd graduated secondary school, but we were just that in love." She beams up at Frank. "Weren't we, honey?"

"Sure were." He leans in and kisses her on the fore-

ONE PUCKING WISH   111

head. "Going to be celebrating thirty years of wedded bliss next month."

Their love and true fondness toward one another radiates from them, bringing a smile to my face and a pain to my chest. What must it be like to know a love like that? Maybe I did know a love like that. Was that what I would've had with Tucker had I not insisted on breaking it off after high school? The time I dated Tucker felt very much like true love, and I can't help but wonder if I'll ever feel it again. Did I ruin my one shot at a lifetime of love? Images of my one and only love and his Target model girlfriend pop into my mind, and the pain in my chest grows.

Gunner nudges my arm. "Frank asked you a question," he says under his breath.

I pull my thoughts from my lost love and refocus my attention on Frank and Alice. "I'm sorry. What did you say?"

"I asked if your parents live in Michigan. That's where your team is from, right?" Frank asks.

I nod. "Yeah, we're from Michigan, but no, my parents are no longer there." I leave it at that because the whole story seems like too much to get into.

Frank doesn't question me further. "What about you?" he asks Gunner.

"Same," Gunner states. The single word makes it clear the discussion is over.

I steal a glance at him and wonder if his parents are no longer alive, like mine, or if they're just not in the picture. Chances are that question will go unanswered as Gunner's demeanor makes it pretty clear that he won't be in the mood to share anytime soon. It doesn't matter anyway. Whatever relationship Gunner has with his parents is none of my business. Once we leave here, everything will go back to the way it was, and this version of ourselves will cease to exist.

But still…I can't help my curiosity. Something in Gunner's expression and the abruptness in which he answered makes me want to question further.

We finish eating, and Alice clears our plates. We thank her again. Admittedly, I feel like a new person after the meal—one who isn't starving—and it's a relief.

Alice waves me forward. "I wanted to show you something."

I turn to Gunner, but he's looking away with a blank stare. I don't bother saying anything as it's clear he won't miss my absence. Alice leads us toward a room in the back of their place. It has shelves of plastic bins on one side of the room and hooks piled with coats on the other. There are cubbies filled with shoes and a door that leads outside.

She gives me a warm smile. "I know you said no, but I wanted to offer one more time." She motions toward the bins and the labels affixed to the outside of them, which I now see are labeled with sizes. "I have about ten different sizes of clothes in these things. I've been a yo-yo dieter all my life, so I always keep all sizes of my clothing. However, I've maintained this weight for a few years now and have decided it's time to donate this lot. So please feel free to take anything you want. As I said, it's all going to be donated anyway. You just don't look comfortable, my dear."

"Oh, okay." I stumble on my words, still processing what she's saying.

She continues, "If I'm overstepping, I apologize. I just wanted you to know that we have options. As a woman who has been too many sizes to count, I know that clothing sizes can be an awkward subject."

I take Alice in and can't imagine her looking any other way than how she does now. And I do appreciate the thought behind this gesture. "Thank you, Alice. This is really sweet of you."

With final instructions insisting that I take whatever I want, she shuts the door that separates this room from the rest of her home and leaves me with the bins of clothes. Grabbing the one labeled with my current size, I open the lid and pull out a few pairs of leggings, T-shirts, a warm-looking sweatshirt, and a zip-up hoodie. I hope that we're not going to be here long enough for me to need all of these items, but I take them just in case.

Clothes slung over my arm, I exit the mud room to find Gunner standing with his arms crossed and a scowl on his face, waiting for me. He's evidently had enough socializing and is ready to return to the room.

I ignore the six-foot-five man and his heated stare. I'm thinking a change of pace is in order for today.

"Do you have any playing cards we can borrow?" I ask Alice.

"Sure, sweetie." She hurries to the cupboard in the living area, opens the door, and retrieves a deck of cards. "You're not going to like them, though," she says, placing the deck in my hands.

I look down at the playing cards and smile. The deck has the blue orca in the shape of the letter C, the Vancouver Canucks logo. "Oh...Alice." I shake my head. "You just made my job of convincing that one"— I nod toward Gunner—"to play card games with me a lot more difficult."

She shrugs, her lips tilting into a wide smile. "What can I say? You're in Canuck territory."

CHAPTER TEN

GUNNER

I stare into Penny's pleading eyes. "No," I repeat, my voice firm.

Penny has either been in my T-shirt or naked for the past day and a half, and at this moment, she is neither. Instead, she's wearing some clothes from Alice, and while they look comfortable, I want them off her. They're definitely something Alice would wear, but I'm not a fan.

"Come on. It will be fun," Penny says for the tenth time.

"I'm not a card game person," I state once more.

While our entertainment choices are limited, playing a goofy game of cards is the last thing I feel like doing. I'd rather stare at a wall than see how many cards I can collect in the same suit. The process sounds horrid. Penny insists that we should take a break from all the sexual activity today, and quite frankly, I think that sounds like an incredibly stupid idea.

In fact, the thought of not ripping that sweatshirt off Penny has me feeling on edge—inexplicably angry even. Surely, the roads will be cleared by tomorrow. Canada has to be used to snow. It's not as if three feet of snow was dumped on Florida or Texas. We're in the north, where people can handle snow and ice. Getting things back to normal around here shouldn't take more than two days. Deep down, I'm very aware that this time with Penny is coming to a close, and that thought fills me with rage.

The amount of unease I feel is unsettling. I should be ecstatic that we get to go home soon, and I can't figure out why I'm not. Yes, sex with Penny is good. Hell, it's fucking great. But I've had plenty of great sex in my life. That can't be it. Routine has always been my safe space. The thought of getting back to my place, the team, lifting, practice, and games should bring me a sense of calm. Yet it's doing the opposite.

Add in the fact that playing nice with Penelope Stellars takes a lot of energy. Small talk and pleasantries are not my thing, either. However, the two of us agreed to be different people while we're here—ones who don't hate each other. Surprisingly, I'm doing just that. I should be thrilled that soon enough, I can be myself. Yet once again… I'm not.

It makes no sense.

I'm in need of some major stress relief, which would explain why I want to tear Penny's clothes from her body. But no. The cool girl who was down for fucking all day long yesterday has been replaced with the rummy card game pusher.

"Fine." She sighs. "What do you want to do?" I open my mouth to speak, and she cuts me off, holding a finger up. "That's not sexual in nature."

Seriously, where is yesterday's Penny?

"I don't know," I grumble.

She taps her thumbs across her phone. "No flights yet but they're thinking tomorrow. I can't wait to get home."

"Same," I lie.

I sit against the headboard, and Penny sits cross-legged, facing me. "Well, if you don't want to play rummy, which I think is a bad call, I guess we can talk. Seeing that we're still here in this fake friendship, I guess we could get to know each other. I mean, all I know about you is that you're huge, a great goalie, and kind of an ass."

I lift my shoulders. "That sums me up."

"Back at Frank and Alice's, you said you didn't have any family in Michigan, but—"

I cut her off. "No."

"What do you mean no?"

"I mean, we're not doing that," I scoff. "We're not having any heart-to-hearts or whatever. I don't do that shit."

"What shit? Talking about yourself? Your family?"

"Exactly."

"What about with your friends and the team? You don't ever share with them?" she questions.

I shake my head. "No, first of all, my only friends are the team. Second, sharing isn't my thing."

She blows out a breath. "Okay, well, where do your parents live if not Michigan?"

"No."

"Are they alive?"

"I said no," I state more firmly.

She rolls her eyes. "Okay, so…we can't talk about ourselves. You won't play a card game with me. What do you want to do, then?"

"You know what I want to do."

Her brows furrow as a scowl finds her face. She drops the deck of cards onto the bed and stands. Hands on her hips, she paces back and forth over the narrow pathway between the bed and the bathroom. "I don't want to do that anymore," she says finally.

"Why?" The question comes out loudly.

She turns her palms toward the ceiling in an annoyed gesture. "I don't know. I just don't."

"You seemed to enjoy it the night we got here and all day yesterday. I thought our arrangement was working. What changed?"

"It just started to feel like…"

"Like what?"

She shakes her head. "I don't know."

"You don't know, or you won't say?" I hold her stare in mine.

"I don't know," she says quietly.

"Fine," I huff out. "Get over here. I'll play your stupid card game."

I don't believe her for one second. She's not telling me something, but I can't fault her for it. I'm not telling her anything. If there's one thing I understand, it's wanting to keep your thoughts and feelings to yourself. So I'll give her that.

Sitting here all day, stuck in this room, doing nothing more than twiddling our thumbs, will make me go insane. If my only option is playing cards, then so be it.

"Really?" She looks at me with a raise of her brow.

"Yeah." My barely audible response mirrors my lack of enthusiasm.

She reclaims her position across from me on the bed

and starts shuffling the cards. After dealing us each five cards, she places the rest of the stack, which is apparently now the draw pile, between us and goes over the rules. The game isn't rocket science. We collect groups of cards for points, either same suit cards or runs like three, four, five or jack, queen, king. At the end of each hand, we add up our points and play again.

I've never been into games. It's just not my thing. This one, in particular, presents no real challenge. A child could play it. I don't see the draw of spending time in this way. Yet I keep my opinions to myself. Spending the rest of the time we're stuck here fighting isn't the desired outcome.

"We used to always play until someone reached five hundred points, but we can play to any number, really." Penny lays down three aces in front of her.

I draw a card from the stack and put the single ace in my hand into the discard pile.

"Rummy!" Penny slaps the pile and picks up the discarded ace. "Remember, if you have something in your hand that you can play off one of my cards, you can place it down in front of you and earn the points on that."

"Got it."

Penny draws a card and bites her lip as she stares at the cards in her hands. I can almost see the wheels in her head turning, trying to figure out her next move. At this moment, she looks young and precious—a far cry from her badass, tough-as-nails businesswoman persona she normally wears. The red ringlets that fall in front of her shoulders and her perfect, makeup-free skin add to the illusion of innocence. Truthfully, it's hard to believe the woman I know is the same one sitting across from me.

"I never pictured you as a card game type of person," I say.

She shrugs. "I haven't played in probably ten years. I used to play all the time with someone when I was young. He loved card games." She grins.

"An old boyfriend?"

"We were friends first, but then, yeah, we dated."

"And you broke up?" This room must be enchanted because not only do I barely recognize Penny, I don't recognize myself. Who is this man asking questions about an old boyfriend?

She pins me with a stare. "No, we're still together. I should probably remind him of that since he just proposed to someone else."

"Very funny," I deadpan. "Well, it sounds like you're still friends, then."

She shakes her head. "No, not really. I mean, I'm forced to attend his wedding this summer. I went to a small high school and my entire graduating class will be there. Considering how close Tucker and I were, people would notice if I wasn't there."

"Do you want to go to the wedding?"

"No."

"Because you still have feelings for him?"

She scoffs. "No because I don't care about any of those people anymore. That part of my life is in the past."

"Then don't go."

"Easier said than done."

I shrug. "Not really. It's really easy not to do something you don't want to do."

She pulls her eyes from her cards and holds my stare. "Why do you care? In fact, why are you asking all these questions? Aren't you the one who doesn't want to talk about anything?"

"I don't care." I lean back against the headboard, the features of my face, unmoving.

"Well, if you keep asking me questions, expect the same. Tit for tat. It's only fair," she says.

"I'll save you the trouble. No, I never played rummy with an ex-boyfriend, and no, I won't be attending any weddings this summer."

"I get to pick the questions."

"I don't think so."

She drops the pile of cards in her hand onto the discard pile. "This sucks. Doesn't it?"

"Yeah." I follow suit and toss the cards in my hand atop hers. "It does."

"Can you put those away?" She nods to the playing cards. "I'm going to make some calls."

Grabbing her phone, she heads into the bathroom and closes the door.

Mascots are weird, I think as I put away the teal and royal blue cards. Who chooses a weird-looking whale in the shape of the letter C as their mascot? Then again, we have a frail Sandhill Crane, a bird that wouldn't win in a fight against a squirrel, as ours.

I toss the package of stupid cards, and they land atop a big box of toilet paper before sliding to the floor. Blowing a breath, I position my arms behind my neck and lie back on the bed. Penny chatters away in the bathroom as I stare at the ceiling. I'm so antsy and ready to get out of this room and back home. It was fine for the first day and a half when it consisted of loads of hot sex. But now, I'm officially over it.

Penny takes forever, talking on the phone in the bathroom. Unable to stare at the ceiling any longer, I make my way to the bathroom and open the door just as Penny places her phone on the countertop.

"Any news?" I ask.

"Yeah, we're out of here tomorrow morning." She grins and releases a sigh of relief. "It's costing the Cranes a significant amount of money to charter a plane for us, but there is nothing commercial for several days. Every flight is booked with an extensive standby list from all the passengers with canceled flights over the past two days. But"—she looks at me with a smile—"our bosses want *the Beast* back before we play Florida, and they're willing to pay."

"Good," I huff. "I'm starting to go a little crazy."

"Weren't you already crazy?" she teases, and once again, I have to remind myself who this woman is. All the different sides of her I've seen over the past two days are making me dizzy.

"Funny," I say without emotion. "All right...we just have to get through one more night of being stuck in this room."

She nods. "Yeah." The single word comes out hesitant. She pulls in a breath before abruptly huffing out, "Fine."

My brows furrow. "Fine, what?"

"Let's do it."

"Do it?"

"You know exactly what I mean." She rolls her eyes. "It's our last night here. Instead of sitting in silence and staring at cardboard, let's do it. Because tomorrow..."

"Everything goes back to the way it was." I finish her sentence.

"Exactly."

"Are you sure? We don't have to. We can play your stupid card game again."

She crosses her arms in front of her and tugs at the hem of the sweatshirt, pulling it up and over her head. Braless, she stands before me naked from the waist up. My body tenses, and burning-hot lust courses through me, leaving me hard with desire.

"There are some additional rules this time," she says as she shimmies out of the leggings. "Nothing sweet or romantic. I don't want you to tell me how perfect my body is or anything like that. In fact, let's keep the talk to a minimum. And no oral. Just sex. I just want hard, rough sex. I want to feel good, come, and then go to bed so tomorrow we can leave this place. Deal?"

Is she kidding with this? She just gave me a free pass to fuck her. No response needed. She knows exactly where I stand. My clothes find the floor in record time. I grab Penny's waist and turn her away from me so she's facing the bathroom mirror. The palm of my hand splays against the skin of her back, and I push her toward the bathroom counter.

She steps to the side, widens her stance, and leans her forearms against the counter. Her heated stare finds mine in the mirror, and we both moan in unison as I slide into her from behind.

My fingers dig into her hips as I pull her ass against

me and enter her hard and rough. Her breasts bounce against the counter as I thrust into her over and over again.

The sounds of our skin slapping and our pleasure-laced moans fill the space. The sight of Penny in the mirror and the skin of her chest a flush of red as I take her from behind is pure fucking heaven. She feels so good. I hook my forearms under her thighs and lift her legs so I can go deeper. Tightening my leg muscles, I use them to pound into her hard, and she screams.

"Like that?" I groan.

Her mouth hangs agape as she releases soft moans. Her eyes are hooded, and her face is heavy with plea-sure. She nods, closing her eyes, and I thrust into her again and again, giving her everything I have until her body is shaking and she's crying out.

With a final thrust, my chest falls against her back as my own orgasm hits, and I empty inside her.

I gave her exactly what she wanted. It was hard, rough, and I know I made her feel good. Only this is where the plan deviates. I'm not tired, and we're not sleeping just yet. She'll find slumber when she's so sated and boneless that she can't keep her eyes open any longer.

CHAPTER ELEVEN

PENELOPE

I don't think I've ever felt this good. I've had my fair share of sex, and I think I've experienced a vast array of emotions. I've made love with Tucker, and it was perfect at the time. There have been one-night stands and flings that've lasted a couple of weeks or months—and everything in between.

But I've never felt this.

Sex with Gunner is next level. Our bodies fit together so well, one could think that they were made for one another. But I'm not delusional. I know Gunner isn't my soulmate, and we're not compatible outside this motel in Canada. Yet the chemistry is there, at least, when it comes to our physical needs. It's undeniable. And it sucks because after tonight, I'm never going to experience it again.

The way in which Gunner makes me feel has thrown me off over the past two days. To be honest, it's confusing. I shouldn't want him as much as I do, nor should I enjoy sex with him this much either. I tried stopping the madness earlier and putting an end to it. I got the cards and attempted to fill our time with something other than mind-blowing sex, but it was impossible.

We face each other. A sheet covers our naked bodies. Gunner's hand is on my hip, and his tongue is in my mouth. God...he's a good kisser. We've kissed for so long my lips are starting to go numb, but I don't pull away. I can't. Our lips move against one another, and our tongues dance, slow and seductively, as if they've been waiting for this connection forever.

This.

This is what I don't want.

I don't want to feel all of this.

As a pair, we're spent. Gunner rose to the challenge and gave me everything he had. I don't have the energy for another orgasm, and I'm certain he doesn't have the stamina to give me another. We should go to sleep so we can wake up and finally get back to our life. Instead, we kiss and kiss and kiss.

My facial muscles ache, but I don't want to stop. I want this feeling for as long as I can have it.

It's stupid, all of it. A war rages in my mind, a battle between logic and desire. Only, it's not really a battle at all—logic barely put up a fight because this kiss is that good.

Tomorrow, this will all be gone, as it should.

Still, I didn't want this because what we're doing—feels like more. This kiss feels like forever.

Yet with Gunner, there will never be more.

There can't be.

A monstrous truck arrives to pick us up for the airport before the sun rises. I have to give it to the ladies in the Crane office who are making the calls. They found a car service with a vehicle that should be able to make it through the snow.

The driver, a bearded man named Boon, reassures me that most of the main roads have been plowed, so he'll have no problem getting us to the airport. He helps me into the back seat of his truck, the door to which is almost level with my waist. This truck is massive.

I peeked into the motel office right before Boon

arrived to see if Alice or Frank were there, but it was dark. I feel awful leaving without saying goodbye, especially after all they've done for us. I'll make sure to send them a gift basket in a few days as a thank-you.

Gunner hasn't said much since we woke. He's impossible to read so I have no idea what's going on in his head. Perhaps not much, especially if his thoughts mirror mine. I'm exhausted, and all I can really think about is getting back home. Unlike Gunner, I get to go to my condo, plop on the couch, and take a nap. I'm sure he's expected to hit the ice for some practice before tomorrow's game.

Boon is the opposite of our driver Julien from a few nights ago. The main difference is he's not a chatterbox. Besides reassuring me that the roads were passable and double-checking that he was taking us to the correct place, he hasn't uttered a word.

It's refreshing and fits the vibe. Neither Gunner nor myself are in the mood for gab either. The ride is quiet save for the deep rumble of the big truck's engine and the sound of the massive tires crunching over the snow. Not only is the quiet different but so is my probability-of-death meter. Unlike the ride with Julien several days ago, I don't feel as if I might die at any given moment. This feeling of relative safety allows my mind to take in the past few days. I'm perplexed over how things will be between Gunner and me now that he's spent the better part of three nights and two days inside me. That's bound to change our dynamic.

This wasn't a one-night stand, and I fear the fallout isn't going to follow as if it was. What we shared seemed like more, despite us saying it wasn't. I've had one-night stands, but I've never had that level of connection like what I had with Gunner.

We made it clear it was only a Vancouver thing. Neither of us wants anything that happened to carry over to our normal lives. Still… it feels odd. I'm hoping our time will fade into the past where it needs to stay once I get back to my home and routine.

The charter plane is a welcome sight.

After thanking Boon for safely getting us to the tarmac, we board the plane in silence.

The plane is smaller than the one we normally take to games, but Gunner chooses a seat in the same area of the plane as he usually does. I typically sit at the very back, but the thought of hanging in the rear of the aircraft by myself seems strange when it's only the two of us aboard, so I opt to sit in the same row as Gunner but on the other side of the aisle.

"Do you have practice today?" I finally ask after takeoff.

"Yeah." Gunner sighs.

He looks exhausted, and I'm sure he is. I certainly

am. I can't imagine putting in a full workout after landing. When we get home, I'm going straight to bed.

"I'm looking forward to going home and taking a nap," I say with a half-hearted chuckle. "I don't envy you."

"Yeah." His response is the same.

There's no other conversation to be had. After a few minutes, Gunner puts his AirPods in and leans back against the seat, his eyes closed.

I don't initiate any other conversation. We've agreed to go back to the status quo, which means our interactions will be few and far between—and usually unpleasant—like before. A wave of sadness washes over me, and I can't deny that the idea of returning to normal doesn't sit well.

The past few days have changed things somehow. Only we're going to pretend they didn't.

It's all unsettling, but at the same time, it's the only course of action that makes sense. I need to let it go.

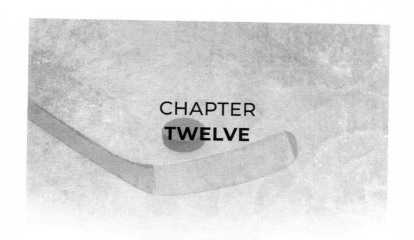

CHAPTER
TWELVE

GUNNER

My mind is half-asleep, but my body moves on instinct as we go through one drill after the next. I could complete these training exercises with my eyes closed. I've been doing this for so long that it's all muscle memory at this point. Despite my body being a little sore, it performs well.

Coach seems happy with my performance in practice. At least I assume he is. There isn't as much yelling as there is when he's pissed. He definitely wasn't pleased that I missed two full days of practice after our loss in Vancouver.

"Do some shooting drills, and you're done," Coach Albright calls out before walking away from the ice.

I take my position in front of the net, and the guys line up on the opposite end of the ice. Cade and Beckett are first, and they skate forward, passing the puck between themselves until Beckett hits it toward me. It goes toward the corner of the net and is easily stopped with a reach of my hand. It hits my glove and bounces back onto the ice.

Beckett skates in front of me. "What should we bet on today?" He likes to make the shooting drills more exciting by turning them into a game.

"No games today, Feltmore," I warn. "Let's just get this done so I can go home."

"Tired after your vacation with spicy Penny, huh? What happened with that? You two hook up or what?" Beckett asks. Cade closes in on the net, clearly eager to get in on the conversation.

"Get to the end of the line," I warn.

"Answer the question, and I'll go." Beckett grins.

"Nothing happened. I'm exhausted from sleeping on a lumpy mattress in a shitty hotel with no access to food because of the storm. It wasn't fun. I'm tired. Let's finish."

The two skate back to the line. They say something to the others, but I can't hear what it is. Bash and Jaden skate down next. Bash tries some new pass that I haven't seen him use before Jaden attempts to hit the puck in.

The puck is stopped, and I smack it out to them with my stick. Instead of turning and skating back, they come forward. Bash speaks first, "Is it true you and Penny had to share a bed?"

"Go," I state.

Jaden chimes in. "There's no way the two of you shared a bed for three nights and didn't bump uglies. Be honest."

I stand tall. "I will kick your ass."

Jaden raises his gloved hands. "Okay. Okay. You know, if you'd be more open in your communication, we wouldn't have to ask so many questions."

I lunge forward. The motion sends Bash and Jaden back to the other end of the ice in record time. They say something to the rest of the team, and whatever it was does the trick because there are no more questions throughout the remainder of the shooting drills. I've never met a group of guys who love gossip more than this one does.

We finish up practice and hit the showers. I hurry out of the locker room at record speed. I came straight here from the airport, and I can't wait to get back to my place.

Pulling into my drive, I park my car and release an audible groan. A gorgeous blonde stands at my front door. The universe is testing my patience today.

It's Felicity, a pharmaceutical rep I've been hooking

up with for a couple of years every time she swings through town. No emotions are involved for either of us; it's just sex. I'm normally happy to see her but not today.

"Surprise," she says when I step onto the porch. "I had an unscheduled trip to Detroit, so I decided to drop by."

I give her a nod and a grunt.

She follows me into the house. "I know we have a sex-only type of relationship, but how long do we have to know each other before you stop communicating in grunts," she teases.

"Just tired, Felicity."

She drags her bottom lip into her mouth and bites it. Lifting a brow, she steps toward me and circles her arms around my neck. "I know how to wake you up." Standing on her tiptoes, she leans in and drags her tongue up my neck until she's nibbling on my earlobe. She splays her palm atop my shirt over my chest and slides it down until she's cupping my cock over my jeans. "How long has it been since the last time? Three months?"

"Something like that."

"I've missed you."

I doubt that. I guarantee Felicity has a sexual partner in every city she visits. She's not pining over our time together when she's away, which is fine because neither am I.

"I'm just not..." She halts my protest with her mouth, shoving her tongue in my mouth.

I've kissed this woman a hundred times, yet this time, it feels strange. Her tongue moves with mine, and it's foreign to the point it's unpleasant.

Memories of soft and supple lips, and intoxicating moans fill my mind, but when I thread my hands through Felicity's thin, straight hair, it feels off. My fingers crave thick locks, and my lips want someone else. Hell, my whole body wants someone else.

I stop the kiss. "I can't."

Felicity takes a step back with an expression of utter shock. "You can't what?"

"Do this with you today."

"I'm only in town for the day, Gunner," she says as if this is all the explanation I need.

I turn away from her and head to the kitchen for a glass of water. "I know. Sorry," I call over my shoulder.

She follows me into the kitchen. "I'm confused. You've never turned me away before. What's going on? Are you seeing someone?"

I down an entire glass of water before answering. "No, I'm not seeing anyone. I just don't want this today."

"You don't want me?" she snaps, her mouth falling agape. "What am I missing here?"

I'm starting to wonder if anyone has ever turned this woman down. She's absolutely smoking hot, great in bed, and truthfully fun to be around. So no one may have.

"Look, I was stuck in Canada for several days in a snowstorm. I was in a crappy motel with no food and shitty sleep. I just got back a couple of hours ago, and I'm exhausted. I need to rest up before our game tomorrow. It's nothing against you, but I need you to go."

"Oh, well... okay." She still looks like she can't believe I'm turning her away. She shrugs. "I guess I'll go. I don't know when I'll be in town next."

Pressing my hand against the small of her back, I lead her to the front door. "Well, you know where to find me when you do."

"Right." She frowns. "See ya."

"See ya." I close the front door on her bewildered expression.

Everything I said to her is true. I do need to rest up for tomorrow. This has nothing to do with Penny. She and I aren't together, nor would I feel guilty about sleeping with someone else. In fact, if Penny showed up at my front door and wanted to sleep with me, I'd turn her away, too. More than likely.

Probably.

No, I'd turn her away.

That was a Vancouver-only situation.

No way can I hook up with Penny again. Definitely not.

CHAPTER
THIRTEEN

PENELOPE

My entire body aches. Each step to my bedroom is more cumbersome than the last. I mentally curse my weak muscles that can barely lift my legs. I can't remember the last time I've felt this tired. This is some soul-deep exhaustion.

The delicious scent of cinnamon, nutmeg, apples, and pumpkin spice greets me when I open my bedroom door, lingering from years of burning nothing but autumn-inspired scented candles. I lift a three-wick candle from my nightstand titled *Autumn Bliss* and take a deep breath.

Now that's what a room should smell like, not must, cardboard, and... *him.*

The memory of Gunner's smell floods my olfactory, pushing away my precious pumpkins.

"No," I protest with a huff of my nose as if the motion is going to push away the scent. Nostrils toward the candle, I inhale deep until I'm back to smelling only perfectly delectable hints of autumn manufactured with chemicals by a scientist in a lab as nature intended it. "That's better."

I return the unlit candle to its home on my night-stand and fall face-first onto my bed. The plush duvet cover with its appropriate thread count feels amazing against my skin. Frank and Alice are great people and obviously did us a huge favor, but in retrospect, their motel, even a room that wasn't a storage closet, would be a two-star on a good day.

Closing my eyes, I all but melt into my pillow-top mattress. My limbs feel boneless, and I'm ready to sleep until tomorrow when I go with the team to Florida for their game against Tampa Bay.

My thoughts go to the past several days and all they entailed. My mind replays everything from the death-defying Uber ride to the stale donuts and hunger pains to my time locked up in that room with the grumpy goalie, and while he was still as moody as ever, I saw a whole different side of his mood—a passionate, sensual, completely gratifying side. My visions, a mere fraction compared to the real thing, cause my skin to pebble and my heart to race.

"No!" I wiggle beneath the covers and pull them up to my chin. Head against my pillow, I clamp my eyes shut and force my traitorous brain to think of something else.

It only makes sense that I would need a minute to decompress. The past several days don't even feel as if it happened in this world or lifetime. It doesn't seem real because prior to Vancouver, there would've never been a time when I would've slept with Gunner, let alone that many times. More alarming yet is the fact that I enjoyed his company for more than the intimate stuff. Vancouver was this inexplicable twilight zone. While it was obviously real and not some dream, it wasn't me...nor was it him. That's not us, not who we are or what we do—together. We don't have toe-curling sex, converse like two people who get along, and we especially don't make out like teenagers or cuddle.

I just need some time to regulate back into reality, and it will all go back to normal. It's already starting to. I think back to Gunner on the plane. He wasn't the same guy I shared a bed with for three nights, but at the same time, he wasn't his dickish self either. Perhaps we both need time to come out of the snowed-in, lust-filled fog.

My phone chimes at that moment right before sleep pulls me under. I choose to ignore it, and my eyes remain closed. It dings again.

Please stop.

And again.

With a groan, I emerge from my comfy cocoon to silence my phone. Leaving the ringer on was a rookie move, something I never do when I sleep, for good reason. I put the oversight off to utter exhaustion. Despite my better judgment, I check the notification. It's from Iris, and she's informing me that she's here. At my front door.

> Open up!

She texts again.

I release a groan. *Please go away.*

Even as the plea resonates in my mind, I'm throwing the blanket off my body and sitting up because if I know anything about Iris, I know she will not go away. The girl is tenacious, and I suppose one has to be in order to be my friend. I'm not the easiest girl to get close to. A woman with less resolve than Iris would've chalked me up to a lost cause by now, but she keeps showing up… and I love her for it.

With a heavy frown, I open my front door to a wide-smiled Iris.

She shakes her head with a tsk. "Did you think I would leave you to your own devices today after you spent three days alone with Gunner? I just saw him at practice with the team, and he's looking rough." She shoves a cup of Starbucks coffee into my hand. "That's the last one, by the way," she says before stepping inside.

Her words register. "What?" I gasp, looking down at the cup in my hand.

She shrugs. "Yep, that's the last of her mix until pumpkin spiced lattes come back in August."

I can't believe Iris's coffee shop friend didn't stash away more PSL mix. What was she thinking? It's only February, and now I have to wait almost six months. Panic rises, and I recall all the dupe recipes I've tried in the past. A few of them were decent, so I suppose they could work, but none of them were the real deal.

Iris steps in front of me, her face an inch from mine. "Earth to Penny. Did you hear me?"

I blink. "Huh?"

She laughs. "I knew it. Something happened. Gunner looks slow out on the ice, and you can't even answer a simple question. I want to know everything."

Following her into the living room, I take a sip of my coffee. "What are you talking about? I didn't hear your question. I'm in shock over the fact that this is my last PSL of the season."

"You'll live." She grins and plops down on my sofa. "Just think, you got over two more months than everyone else. It's all about perspective, Pen."

I sit at the other end of the couch and turn to face her. "I still think it's stupid they don't offer it year-round."

She rolls her eyes. "Yes, it's a tragedy. Now give me details. What happened in Vancouver? I swear I texted you a hundred times, and you didn't respond. The storm was so horrible we had to leave you there or risk getting stuck ourselves, and then you go radio silent. I didn't know for a whole day whether you found shelter. I was worried sick."

Taking another sip of coffee, I will the caffeine to bring me back to life. "Well, there's not much to tell. The first night was spent trying to find somewhere to stay, and once we found a place, the reception was horrible. Half of my texts and messages didn't load until we were back in the city at the airport days later. I didn't mean to worry anyone. I got ahold of the ladies in the office and figured they could relay the message to the team—that we were snowed in and would get back as soon as we could."

"Well, they did. But that's like zero real information, Penny. I need to know the juicy *details*."

The throw blanket hanging on the back of the sofa catches my eye, and I pull it over my legs before answering Iris. I'm not sure if I'm actually cold or just need an additional barrier between us. Not many people truly know me, but Iris is on the short list of those who know me the most. She's pretty good at reading people, but as much as I adore her, I can't tell her about Gunner and me. I'm not telling anyone. It was a one-off experience, a result of nothing more than boredom. It didn't mean anything and probably should have never happened in the first place. I don't want her making more out of it.

"I don't know what more you want to know. As I told you, we called every hotel in the city, and they were all booked. Frank, the bartender, and his wife own a motel outside the city. It was also full, but they had one room they used as storage, and he offered it to us. So we hung out amid boxes of paper goods and mini-shampoo bottles. On the first day, we basically starved, and the second day, Alice, the co-owner of the motel, fed us. It was long and boring, and I was counting down until we got out of there."

She leans forward, her eyes squinting. "So what was the sleeping situation like? What'd you do all day? What'd you talk about? Did you fight? I mean, you guys hate each other. I just can't picture it. You and him, stuck together for three days."

I shrug. "We called a truce and agreed to get along while we were there. We slept in the bed. There wasn't much talking, just existing, I guess, and waiting out the storm. As I said, it was a boring couple of days."

"You mean 'beds,' right?" She quirks a brow.

Shit.

Schooling my face, I attempt to emit the most unbothered expression I can muster. "There was only one."

"Penny!" she screams, a laugh erupting as she throws her head back. "You shared a bed with the Beast for three nights, and you're telling me nothing happened? At the very least, there had to be some spooning or something."

My features remain stoic. "I don't know what you want me to say. We slept. That's all. This wasn't a chapter from one of those romance novels you love to read. It was real life, and real life is boring. I was stuck in a room with a guy I can't stand. I got through it, and that's all there is to it."

She squints her eyes, puckering her lips, and I swear the woman can see right through me. "You know love and hate are separated by the thinnest of veils. I know how the one-bed thing works. Remember Cade and me in Barbados? That was real life." She holds up her left hand, flashing her diamond ring. "We all see how that turned out."

I roll my eyes. "Completely different. You two have loved each other since you were children. There is no love between me and Gunner. We were stuck in a shitty situation—one that *he* put us in—remember? We called a truce for the sake of our sanity and pretended to tolerate one another for a couple of days, and then we flew home. That's all there is to it." I shrug.

"Really?" Her face falls in disappointment. "You have no juicy details for me?"

"None."

"Why do you both look like death today?" She raises her hands in mock surrender. "No offense."

The corners of my lips tilt up as I fight a smile. "Because we've barely eaten in days and were bored out of our minds stuck in another country, sharing a way-too-small, lumpy bed in a glorified storage closet. It wasn't fun, Iris."

She pouts her lips out in a frown. "Bummer. Did you do anything for your birthdays, at least?"

"We ate stale donuts with sprinkles."

"You really did have a horrible time, didn't you?"

I nod. "We did."

She falls back against the back of the sofa. "I guess I was wrong."

"About?"

"Don't get mad, but I always thought that you and Gunner hated each other so much because you secretly had feelings for or, at the very least, were attracted to one another. I really thought that being stuck in a hotel room with him for three nights would've pulled your feelings out. You know? But it didn't. So I completely misread the situation. I'm usually better at reading people. Then again, I didn't see the whole Beckett and Elena thing either. Nor did I realize that Cade had been waiting for me for all those years." Her face falls, and she sits up. She looks at me, her big blue eyes wide. "I apparently don't know myself at all."

I chuckle. "Don't go having some identity crisis. You are good at reading people. No one saw the situation with your brother and Elena. Who would've guessed that he'd secretly get married to the new team doctor in Vegas so that she wouldn't lose her inheritance only to fall in love with a woman twelve years his senior? Those two are as different as night and day. No one saw that coming."

"Yeah." She grins. "But they are so amazing together. Don't you think? It makes me wonder why I didn't see it before."

"They do seem very happy. And the thing with Cade—you can't count that either. No one can see the full picture when they're in it."

"Yeah, I guess. Still, I really thought I saw something between you and Gunner."

I scoff. "Me and the grumpy goalie? Come on, Iris."

"I know it seems weird, but I saw something there...or, at least, I thought I did."

"Sorry to burst your bubble, but it's time to move on to someone else."

A renewed smile finds her face. "Did you pick up some chemistry between Bash and Ariana at the resort during bye week?"

I laugh. "I didn't mean right now!"

"You said to move on to someone else, so I'm moving on to someone else," she quips.

"Okay, but not now. I'm exhausted. Plus, no. I think Elena would kill any player who tried to get with her daughter."

"Bash is the baby on the team. He's only a couple of years older than Ariana. I think they'd be cute together."

Holding out my hands, I shake my head. "Not in the mood."

"Fine." She sighs. "Well, I have everything set up for meet and greet after the game tomorrow. And, the linen supplier doesn't have enough white tablecloths for the charity dinner next week, so I ordered the cream. I figure it will look just as good with the color scheme we have picked out."

"Iris, you know I love you, but I'm going to have to kill you if you don't leave."

"What?" She giggles.

"I'm tired and need to sleep. I have full confidence in you and all your decisions. If you think hot-pink linens will look best, I trust you. I don't care about who has chemistry with who. And, if I'm being honest, the only reason I'm still sitting here is because I'm enjoying my last few sips of my latte, which I won't have again until August. So I appreciate you stopping by, but can you please leave now?"

She groans in mock annoyance. "Okay, then." She hops up from the sofa. "I'll leave. One of these days, you'll have to give me something juicy. A friendship requires some tea, Penelope."

"I'm not the tea-spilling type of girl. You know that about me."

"I do, and I love you anyway," she singsongs. "Oh, I'm all caught up at work and literally have nothing to do, so I'm taking the rest of the day off to play with Sandy. Okay, boss?"

Sandy is the golden wiener dog that she got Cade for Christmas, and I don't blame her. I'd rather hang out with the puppy than most of the people at work, too.

Bringing the cup to my lips, I take a sip and give her a thumbs-up.

"See you tomorrow," she says before leaving the living room.

The front door closes, and I'm left alone with my coffee and thoughts. I can't believe she thought there was something between me and Gunner. I'm even more sure of my decision not to say anything about our time together in that hotel room. If she had thought there were some hidden feelings there before, our Vancouver escapades would have given her all the fuel she needed to fan that fire. And there's no flame. No fire. No feelings.

There's nothing between me and the grumpy goalie besides a distant memory of an extended one-night stand. Which, if I'm being honest, doesn't even feel real. It felt like a dream. And like all dreams... they're soon forgotten.

CHAPTER
FOURTEEN

GUNNER

It's crazy how one day my feet are so frozen I can no longer feel them, and a couple of days later, I'm sweating in places I didn't even know I could sweat. The humidity in Florida is no fucking joke. My lip—my actual lip—is dripping with beads of sweat.

"Who picked this shithole?" Beckett grumbles to my side before taking a sip of his beer.

I think the bar is supposed to resemble an oversized tiki hut or something. The ceiling is covered in some sort of straw or more accurately palm fronds. The motif is a mix of crap constructed with coconuts or shells. All the furniture is very rustic and very cheap tourist Florida. The space is open to the outside elements, which means it's muggy as hell.

I'd prefer the frozen toes any day. I don't mind the cold. Hell, I willingly spend a good portion of my day on ice. "Probably Cookie," I huff, calling out the youngest member of the team by his much-detested nickname.

"Hey, I resent that," Bash pipes up. "I'm pretty sure it was J-Man."

Jaden joins us with a goofy grin. He's holding a clear fishbowl with bright blue liquid in each hand. The fishbowl drinks have skewers of fruit garnishes and sport a neon drink umbrella. "The Zamboni guy recommended it. His cousin owns it. It's really not bad once you get one of these down." He nods toward the obnoxious drink in his hands. "The drink is called Paradise punch, and for ten bucks, you can get it in a fishbowl." He takes a long swig of the drink. "That's a pretty good deal."

I roll my eyes at the idiot.

"Apparently, it's unseasonably hot for this time of year," Cade says as he and his wife, Iris, join the circle.

"Someplace with air-conditioning would've been great," she adds.

At least we won against Tampa Bay tonight. Had we lost, I'm positive this place and the massive amounts of sweat dripping down my back and into my ass crack would've caused me to lose my mind. The truth is, I got lucky with some of my saves. I wasn't on my A game tonight. Not even close. I felt sluggish as hell. Vancouver really did a number on me. I'm sure the fact that I was off my routine for a few days is the cause.

My eyes dart across the room where the Princess sits in her ridiculous pencil skirt and top made of what I'm certain is the most unbreathable fabric known to man. Long gone are her untamed curls. She's back to the tight, twisted updo. She wears a scowl as her thumbs type across her phone.

I wonder what she's pissed about now.

There's no doubt that sweat is also dripping down into her ass crack. That image plays in my mind, and the familiar pull in my gut resurfaces. No freaking way. I shake my head, willing the images of her sweaty, naked body to vacate my mind. The fact that I actually know what Penelope looks like naked is going to be a problem. It's not hard to brush an urge to the side when that's all it is, but when it's accompanied by very detailed images, it's slightly more challenging. I'm starting to question if our activities, the ones we both agreed to forget about and never speak of again, will pose a problem.

"Hey, do you all remember the last minute of the game? With a flick of the wrist, I sent the puck past Tampa's goalie. The scoreboard lit up." Palms out, Max brings his hands together in front of his face and extends them outward, highlighting the scoreboard in his head. "I mean, I did it for the team, you know?"

Cade bumps his shoulder. "You did good, TJ Maxx. Real good."

Max sighs, a wistful smile on his face. "It was effortless, but sometimes those are the best ones."

I hold in the urge to tell Max to shut his mouth. Cade and Beckett are the leading scorers, so I'll give the defenseman his moment. He earned it, and he's right, it did win the game for us—unlike my pathetic excuses for saves. My head has been stuck in hormone-induced sex with Penny land and not rooted in reality. I really do need to get my shit together.

"This is the year! We're getting that Cup!" Jaden shouts, raising his fishbowl in the air.

Drinks are raised, and the boys start hollering, hyping each other up. I lift my half-empty warm beer and clink the bottle against the others.

"To the Cup!" someone yells.

"To the Cup," I respond in unison with the others.

The spicy, sweet perfume she wears invades my senses, notifying me of her approach before she's said a word.

"Hey, Ms. Stellars." Bash grins in the boy-next-door way that he does. "Can I get you a drink?"

"No, thank you, Sebastian," Penny says from behind me. "I'm going to head out. Does anyone need anything?" The guys verbalize that they don't. "Okay. Well, can I assume since we're the only ones in this place, that you all can handle yourselves appropriately tonight? There will be no issues, right?"

I step to the side and twist so I can see her. Her gaze narrows as she eyes the team.

"You're good to go, boss." Jaden salutes. "We promise to be good."

"Okay," Penny answers, and her voice sounds less than convinced. "Behave," she warns, and she looks directly at me this time.

I set my warm beer on the table and steal a glance as she heads out of the hut, not wanting to make it obvious that I'm watching her.

A very drunk Jaden yaps on about the attributes of the fishbowl drink, and I zone out. I opt to give our after-win team bonding bar outing a few more minutes before calling it a night. I'm exhausted.

A handful of guys wearing Tampa Bay jerseys joins us inside the sweaty tiki hut. From the way they hobble inside, off-balance, I don't think this is the first bar they've frequented. They make a beeline to the bar and down a couple of shots each, yelling obnoxiously after each one.

"I think I'm going to head out," I say to Cade.

"Yeah, I think we are, too," he answers.

"Oh my God, it's the Cranes! Good game, guys!" one of the Tampa fans shouts across the bar.

Beckett gives the Tampa fans a wave and a half-hearted nod. "Yeah, this isn't the vibe. I'd rather be with Elena."

"She back at the hotel?" Max asks.

"Yeah, the pregnancy has her exhausted. Plus, the bar isn't her scene," Beckett says.

"I don't think this bar is anyone's scene," I say. "Well, besides Jaden's." I nod toward my teammate as he holds his fishbowl and dances to a song only he can hear. The guys laugh.

"We should probably get him back to the hotel, too. Any more fishbowls and we're going to be carrying him home. What do they put in that drink anyway?" Cade shakes his head with a laugh.

His wife, Iris, speaks up, "I wonder if it's like the jungle juice we had in college. People just put whatever liquor they had in a big bowl, mixed in some juice and fruit, and called it good. That drink was lethal."

"I wouldn't be surprised if it were similar," Beckett says.

"Hey! It's the Beast!" one of the Tampa fans shouts with a bit of a slur as he comes toward me. "I've been watching you for like ten years, man! I was going to be an NFL goalie. I would've, too, had I not blown out my knee in college." His words run together.

He and his friends stand beside our group now. He continues, holding a fishbowl in his hand. "Wouldn't that have been crazy if I were a goalie and we played against you? I bet I'd be even better than you are."

"Yeah, cool," I state before taking a step back to leave.

"Wait, man! Can I have a picture with you?" he shrieks.

Turning back toward the group, I plaster on what I hope is a smile. "Fine," I say.

"Sweet!" He does a little hop and steps toward me. He stumbles and loses his balance, falling forward. Extending my hands, I hold up his chest as he and his neon-colored drink crashes into me. The cool liquid drenches my front.

"Dude, are you kidding right now?" I push him off me and hold his arms until I'm sure he's not going to fall over.

"Sorry!" he yells.

I look at his friends. "You need to take this one home." I eye their goofy grins and release a sigh. "Call an Uber. I don't think any of you should be driving."

My white T-shirt, now a bright orange, sticks to my chest. Rage at the dumbass laughing hysterically fills me, and I know that's my cue to get out of here. I'm too tired to deal with idiots.

Without another word, I turn and leave.

CHAPTER
FIFTEEN

PENELOPE

G abby has been texting me all day. The RSVPs for Tucker's wedding are due tomorrow, and I haven't sent mine in.

You're going, right?

Everyone is going to be there!

You have to go, Pen!

. . .

Why aren't you answering me?

Who am I going to hang out with at the
wedding if you're not there?

I need my best friend there!!!

Gotta love the three exclamation marks on her last text.
She's always been dramatic, that one. Not to mention,
can we still claim our best friend status if we haven't
seen one another in over five years? I'm thinking not.

I haven't been purposely ignoring her. It's been a
busy day. Road games are always a cluster. I planned
on texting her back at that tiki hut bar. In fact, I opened
my phone to do so when another text came through.
Only this one wasn't from her.

Jammies on, I lean against the headboard of the
hotel bed and stare at my phone.

Nelly... please tell me you're coming.
Haven't gotten your RSVP yet.

There's only one person on earth who has ever called me Nelly. The nickname takes me back to the land of nostalgia and heartache.

I haven't received an actual text from Tucker in a few years. We leave basic comments on social media posts every now and again, and there have been a few DMs on Instagram over the years. They're never deep, usually generic pleasantries reminding the other that we're still alive. There's been no communication via text, so the fact that he reached out to me through my phone number seems much more personal. Add in the name he's been calling me since third grade, and I'm a deer in headlights. I stare at the message, unable to respond. All I can do is read the two sentences over and over again.

I can hear his voice say the words, *Nelly... please tell me you're coming*, and I'd be lying if I said it didn't pull at my heartstrings. I loved Tucker, and I owed everything to him. He was my constant in a world of chaos. He allowed me to be someone other than the daughter of the town drunk. He never made me feel less than and was the perfect boyfriend. Before we were more, he was my best friend. The truth is, I don't know if I miss Tucker or the idea of him. I'm not certain I even know who he is anymore. He definitely doesn't know me. I'm not the same girl I was in high school. I'm assuming that after a life in the military and in the eight years since graduation, he's changed, too.

Nostalgia is a crazy thing. It has me missing a memory that more than likely is no longer real.

Though, when I really stop to think about it, it's not seeing him that has me hesitating. It's the thought of him seeing me. What will he think? Part of me wants him to remember the girl I was just like I remember the boy he was—and leave it as that. What if our current realities don't measure up to our memories? What if he looks at me and questions what he ever saw in me in the first place? It's stupid because it doesn't matter. He's getting married. It shouldn't matter what he thinks of my physical appearance or anything else.

I pull in a deep breath. One thing I've never wanted to be is a coward, and I refuse to be one now.

My thumbs move across the screen as I answer him back.

> Of course I'm coming. I wouldn't miss it for the world. Sorry for the late RSVP. It's been crazy at work.

His response is almost immediate.

> Great. I can't wait for you to meet Marcela.

It takes me a second to remember Marcela is the Target model's name. I scanned the wedding invitation for a total of two seconds before tossing it in my mail basket, never to look at it again. Another text comes through.

> Will you be bringing a date?

> Yes, please.

No problem. Steak, fish, or chicken?

Two steaks, please.

Got you down. See you soon.

And with that, our text exchange is over. I don't have anyone to bring, but even via text, I couldn't admit it. Additionally, I probably wouldn't have chosen the steak if I'd taken a second to think about it. I chose the most expensive one to what... stick it to... the Target model's rich parents? *I have issues.*

"Ugh!" I groan and fall to the side, plopping onto the bed.

After a minute, I pick up my phone and type out a text to Gabby.

I'm going. Just spoke with Tucker. See you there.

. . .

Yay!!!!!!!!!!!

The amount of exclamation points she uses makes me want to scream into my pillow. So I do.

The plane lands back in Michigan, and Iris and I wait for the players and the rest of the occupants to deplane before we follow them out.

"I'm going to run to my parents' to check on Sandy, and I'll be back," she says.

"Take your time. We don't have much to do today," I say.

The guys head off to the locker room to change for practice, and I make my way up to my office. After setting my purse down on my desk, I turn to my fancy coffee maker and hit the button. The water and coffee pod are waiting and ready. I find it best to have it all set up before coffee is needed to alleviate any caffeine emergencies. I grab my favorite flavored creamer from the mini-fridge and pour some into the cup of freshly brewed coffee.

I take a sip. It's no Starbucks PSL, but it's pretty damn good.

Reaching into my purse, I switch my phone off Airplane Mode. The second it has a signal, there is one notification ting after the next.

This can't be good.

Reluctantly, I set my coffee down on my desk and pull up my phone notifications.

"You've got to be fucking kidding me!"

I scan one post after the next and read all the articles I can find.

Jolting up from my chair, phone in hand, I hurry toward the locker room. I burst through the door and approach the bane of my existence. "Dreven, in my office. Now."

He furrows his brows and shoots me a glare. "No. We're practicing."

"Now." I turn on my heels and head back toward my office. The guys tease Gunner as he follows me.

Once we're in my office, I close the door behind him and shove the phone against his chest. "Want to tell me what this is about? You couldn't go one night? Why? Why do you make my job so hard? Do you know what a mess this is going to be to clean up!" My voice is shrieky, and I sound like I'm on the verge of a meltdown, which, if I'm being honest, maybe I am.

Gunner stares at my phone, his eyes narrow. "That fucker."

"Oh yeah? He's the fucker?"

He looks at me. "This isn't what happened! He tripped and fell into me. I caught him and helped him stand."

"Really because your face looks like you're about to kick his ass, and your hands are splayed across his chest like you're shoving him," I snap.

"He had just spilled a fishbowl of icy, sticky liquid all over me. Sorry if I'm not smiling like a fucking Cheshire cat, but I did not push him. I caught him."

"The picture looks like you're attacking him!"

He takes a step toward me, his features schooled. He places the phone on my desk and lowers his voice. "I don't care what the photo looks like. I'm telling you right now, I didn't do shit to that guy besides stopping him from falling onto the floor and smashing his face in. This picture has been taken out of context. Ask all of the guys. I didn't do anything to that idiot. In fact, given the circumstances, I was incredibly patient."

My anger dissipates. "It looks bad, Gunner."

He shrugs. "Maybe so but that doesn't mean that it was."

"And now the guy in Vancouver has come forward saying you hit him, too."

"What? The little dweeb we paid off? The one who got box seats and all the money in my wallet?"

I sigh. "Yeah, that one. I haven't transferred the tickets to him yet, so he won't be getting those. But your cash? That's gone."

"I don't care about the money, Penny. I'm pissed at the fact that he agreed to one thing and did something else."

I throw up my hands. "Yeah, well... welcome to my life, Gunner. Every day is another disappointment. I leave you guys early one time, and this happens." I glare at the image on my phone.

"I told you..."

I nod. "I know, but that's not going to matter. The picture is pretty damning, and now with the Vancouver guy chiming in... it's just not going to go away easily."

"I should've let him fall and break his nose against the floor," Gunner huffs.

I shake my head. "People do all sorts of messed-up things for money. You know he made money with that shot. I mean, it looks awful. The headlines are all over the place, but the one constant is they all paint you in a very bad light." I wave my hand through the air. "Go to practice. I'll figure it out."

Gunner looks like he wants to say something, but instead, he turns and leaves without saying another word.

My coffee is lukewarm now, but I suck it down as if my life depends on it. I need my brain awake. I take a seat at my desk and open my laptop. Grabbing a legal pad of paper and a pen, I start writing out my to-do list.

So much for an easy day.

The sun has long set before I'm satisfied with my day's work. I sent a message to Gunner, requesting he come back to my office. He left for home hours ago, but I don't feel remotely guilty for making him come in. This is his mess after all.

"You summoned," he grumbles, opening my office door.

"Take a seat." I motion toward the chair facing my desk. "We have some stuff to go over."

He does as instructed. "Did you get it all figured out?"

"Well, I sent a letter to the guy in Vancouver threatening to sue him for breach of contract. That night, I had him e-sign a general agreement that I keep on my phone for cases like that. I doubt it will actually hold up in court, just as I doubt the Crane Organization would ever take it to court, but the little jerk doesn't. I think the letter scared him enough, though. He apologized and agreed to withdraw his statement. As for the guy in Florida, he states he didn't say anything negative about you, only sold the picture and the tabloids ran with their own stories. I contacted all media outlets with an official statement from the Crane Organization clarifying what happened last night and what is happening in the photo. Some may run a revised story, but most probably won't. So let's just hope something bigger and better happens in the sports and entertainment world tomorrow that will pull the tabloids' focus away from your photo. In the meantime, I've set up a pretty rigorous tour to brighten your image." I hand him the five-page document.

"A tour?" he holds the packet in his hands.

"Yeah, we'll call it your good deeds tour. I've looked at your schedule for the next couple of weeks, and when you're not training, traveling, or playing, you'll be doing something to improve your image. I have all sorts of volunteer activities set up, which will all involve photo ops, of course. You'll find your schedule, along with your obligations, in your packet."

Gunner flips through the pages. "Are you kidding? This is a shit ton of work, Penny."

"Yeah, well, we have a lot of damage control to do."

"I didn't do anything in Florida to warrant this." He sucks in a breath through his nose.

Splaying my hands on my desk, I lean in. "Look, I get that, but it doesn't matter. It still looks bad for the Crane Organization. That photo, paired with all the hotheaded shit you've done over the years, has created this bad reputation around you, and the owners aren't happy. This good deeds tour is long overdue. It's not just about the photo. If that were an isolated incident, it wouldn't be as bad, but you know it wasn't."

"I don't have time for this shit, Princess."

We're back to using my most despised nickname, making my tiny bit of empathy for the guy dissipate in record time. "Yeah, well, neither do I, yet... here we are. I'm forced to do all this crap with you, set up the photo ops and get the stories in the hands of the news outlets. It's a lot of extra work I wish I didn't have to do either."

He gives me a look that resembles remorse as if he feels bad for adding more to my plate, but that can't be it. That isn't something Gunner Dreven would feel. Yet there's this energy in the room. It's more than remorse. There's a longing, too. Or maybe I'm reflecting my own feelings outward.

Sitting across from Gunner in this office has me feeling things I shouldn't be feeling. The knowledge that most everyone has gone home for the day and we're alone has me on edge. It has emotions from our time together fighting for air, but I shove it all down, suffocating every single one of them.

I cross my legs. Leaning my elbows on the desk, I steeple my hands, pressing my fingers against my lips. "Do you have any more questions?"

Gunner's chest rises and falls, heavier than usual. His tongue peeks out, wetting his lips.

It dawns on me that this is the most we've spoken since we've been back, and I realize I want him to have questions because I don't want him to leave. This is an excuse to talk to him, something I don't normally have. We agreed to go back to the way it was, and that means that the only time we communicate is when he does something to piss me off.

Today has been busy as hell. I've worked nonstop to smooth everything over and set up the plan in his hands. Despite the long hours, it's been a good day. I feel… content, and now I'm wondering why.

He has yet to answer my question, so I ask him another. "Is there something you want to say, Gunner?" Something you want to talk about?"

My question is met with more silence as he runs his palms over his jean-clad thighs. There is contemplation in his gaze. He wants to say something, and he's deciding whether he should.

Abruptly, he pushes himself up from the chair and takes a step away from the desk. He holds the packet up and shakes it. "No. Everything I need to know is right here."

And then he's gone.

I pull in a deep breath and look around my vacant office. Pressing my hand to my chest, I attempt to dull the ache. I can't pinpoint the source of my unease, but it's there, and I wish it wasn't.

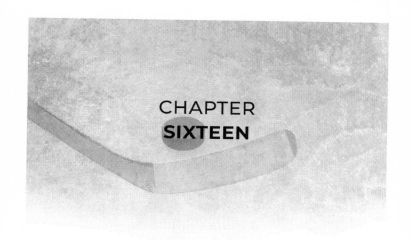

CHAPTER
SIXTEEN

GUNNER

The Gunner Dreven Good Deeds tour is getting old. Penny has been a pain in my ass for weeks now, scheduling one thing after another to prove I'm not the asshole I am. The fact that the photo that caused this all was fabricated is icing on the cake. Though, I suppose it doesn't matter. I may not have shoved the guy in Florida, but I've put my hands on more than a few douches in my day as the Crane goalie. Maybe, as she said, this tour is overdue. Regardless, I'm ready for it to be over.

Not only do we have a several-day break in our play schedule but we've also had a rare stretch of warmer days for March. Something that Penny has made sure to take advantage of. The past two days have included the entire team as we work under our nonprofit building company Cranes Cares. Admittedly, the project is pretty cool. One of the animal rescues in Detroit acquired some land from a generous donor and is building a second kennel so they can take in more dogs. The kennel is almost finished, and it's a beautiful facility. The team is putting the finishing touches on the place today. We're installing the light fixtures, kennel doors, and outside fencing. By the time we leave tonight, they'll be ready for their grand opening this weekend.

Yesterday morning consisted of digging holes, mixing concrete, pouring the concrete into the hole, and placing the metal posts in said concrete. Now that the concrete has dried, we're attaching the chain-link fence to the posts to create a run for each kennel.

"Where did the other pair of pliers go?" I ask Max.

He works on his section of the fence. "I don't know, man." He looks around. "I think I saw J-Man with a pair a minute ago."

I pull off my work gloves and drop them to the ground. "It's fine. I saw a couple of pairs in a toolbox in the supply closet."

On the way back to the kennel, I roll my shoulders and bend my head to each side, stretching my stiff neck. This project has me using muscles I'm not used to working. It probably doesn't help that I've barely taken a break in two days. I didn't want to risk the press snapping a picture I wasn't in. This is all to clean up my image, after all. The cameras have all gone since our project is reaching completion, and I feel a sense of relief.

The toolbox sits on a shelf in the back of the large walk-in closet. Opening the metal lid, I riffle through it for another pair of pliers.

Someone enters the closet, and I don't have to turn around to know it's her. The air in the space changes when she enters.

"I just need to find the light bulbs," she grumbles.

A clear Tupperware bin of light bulbs sits on the top shelf to my right. "These?" I nod toward the bin as I turn around to face her.

"Yes. Can you hand them to me, please?" She stares up at me with her wide doe eyes.

I take her in; my gaze scans her from top to bottom. I'm glad to see she's ditched her usual uniform of a tight skirt and a fancy blouse. However, her pants and top are still more appropriate for an office than a worksite. The heels she wears not only look incredibly uncomfortable but they also make her at least two inches taller. And that damn twist of her hair.

"Why didn't you wear something more comfortable to work in?" I ask.

"Why are you asking me questions about my attire instead of handing me the light bulbs?" she snaps.

Leaving the plastic bin in its place on the top shelf, I take a step toward her. "Why don't you ever wear your hair down or in anything other than this twist?" The question leaves my lips before I can stop it. It was an intrusive thought that I had no right voicing, evident by her appalled gasp. But what's done is done, and at this point, I'm committing to wherever this line of questioning takes me.

"Are you serious right now? Give me the damn light bulbs, Dreven," she orders, her brows furrowed.

"Princess, I just want to know. Doesn't your head hurt with the hair wound so tightly like that all the time?"

"Do not call me that," she warns under her breath.

I take another step toward her. "Do you ever think about Vancouver?"

She's utterly shocked. "No! I don't. And neither should you. Now give me the light bulbs or move so I can get them myself."

I take a step to the side, allowing her to pass. Her heels click against the tiled floor as she hurries past me. She reaches for the shelf over her head, but it's just out of grasp. Stepping up behind her, I grab her waist and lift her.

Shrieking, she hits my arms. "Oh my God, what are you doing? Put me down!"

"I'm helping you reach them."

She kicks her leg back, and her pointy heel goes into my shin. I grunt when the burst of pain hits me. "Put me down, now," she seethes.

This time, I do as instructed. Only, I don't step back. Leaning my arms against the metal shelving, I cage her in.

She turns to face me. "What are you doing? Most days, I can't get two words from you, and the ones I get aren't very nice. Now, you're asking me about Vancouver and picking me up. What the hell is going on, Dreven?"

Maybe I'm going insane, or maybe being alone with her in this small space is doing something to me. I can smell her perfume and the shampoo she uses on her hair. Images of her curly red locks falling over her bare shoulders and ample breasts have me instantly hard.

What. The. Fuck?

"Take your hair down," I order, my voice heavy with need.

"What? No." Her response is firm, but her voice shakes, and she doesn't move.

It's not just images of her hair flashing through my mind. Every minute we were together in Vancouver plays in my head like a highlight reel. Images that I've worked to bury deep explode in my mind in full color, and I'm insane with need—for her. It's almost painful, this desire. An ounce of rational thought left in me tells me to walk away, but I ignore it in favor of every other part of me that wants to stay.

"The hair. Now."

This time, she listens. Her full lips part as she breathes heavy. Lifting her arms, she removes a clip from her hair. It falls from the twist and tumbles down over her shoulders.

I thread my fingers through her hair, running them along her scalp as I shake her curls loose. She closes her eyes and releases a soft moan. Leaning in, I press my lips against hers. I slide my tongue between her lips, requesting access, and she grants it. As my tongue slides into her mouth, her body melts against mine. Our tongues twist as our lips devour one another. With each little whimper that slides from her mouth into mine, my need for her grows.

"Tell me to take off your shirt," I order against her lips.

"Take off my shirt."

I move my mouth from hers and stare at her, fasci-nated. She leans against the shelf, her eyes closed as her chest rises and falls with heavy breaths. I unbutton her blouse. I splay my hands against her soft skin and move my hands up her torso, over her bra, and to her shoulders until her shirt falls to the ground.

"Lock the door," she pants as my fingers burn circles over her skin.

"Yeah. Tell me to take off your bra."

"Take it off."

The second her bra falls, my mouth is on one nipple while my hand tugs at the other.

She threads her fingers through my hair, holding my head against her chest as I suck. "We have to hurry."

I release her nipple with a final flick of my tongue. "Take off your pants," I say as I unzip mine.

"This is stupid. We should stop," she says as she wiggles out of her slacks and panties, leaving her completely bare.

"It is, and we should." I dip my hand between her legs and slide my finger inside. "Tell me to stop."

"No." Her voice shakes as I work my finger inside her, my thumb giving attention to her bundle of nerves.

"This isn't Vancouver, Penny."

"I know."

"This changes things."

She clings to my forearms as her body starts to tremble. "I know."

"Tell me what you want," I whisper into her ear as her body shakes hard.

"Make me feel," she whines.

I rub her clit with a little more force, and she explodes. My free hand covers her mouth as she falls over the edge into oblivion, coming all over my fingers. Removing my hand, I circle both my hands under her ass and lift her. Her legs wrap around my hips as I slide into her. Turning us toward the back of the closet, I push her against the back wall and thrust inside her. She feels so good. I've never had better. Something about Penny is utterly intoxicating.

I bury my face into her neck and pound into her. Clamping my mouth shut, I hold in my sounds. Stars burst behind my eyelids as I explode inside her.

We stay connected in this embrace as I come down from my orgasm. God, that was fucking good.

Penny's eyes go wide as she looks over my shoulder. I whip my head around just in time to see Bash slamming the door shut.

"Fuck," I groan, sliding out of Penny. Her legs unwrap from my hips, and her feet hit the floor.

She pushes my chest and hurries around me, snatching her clothes off the floor. "I told you to lock the damn door!" she whisper-yells.

"No, you didn't. You told me that you locked the door."

She furrows her brows and glares. "What? No, I said, *lock the door*."

"No, you said, *I locked the door*."

She makes quick work of dressing. "I never said I."

"Yes, you did."

"I know I didn't because I knew that I didn't lock the damn door, Gunner. It's why I told you to lock it!" She runs her palms against her head, pulling her hair back tight before twisting it up and securing it with the clip. "I can't believe this is happening. This was so stupid. What were we thinking?"

"I'm going to kill that little shit." I button my jeans.

"You better make sure he doesn't tell anyone. I could lose my job and, worse, my pride. Ugh, I am so stupid!" She smooths her hand over her shirt and again over her hair.

"I'll take care of it," I say.

"You better."

I nod toward the bin of light bulbs. "You want those light bulbs now?"

"No. I'm heading straight to my car and getting the hell out of here. I'm going home to take a long bath and forget this ever happened." She points her finger my way. "Fix this."

With that, she's gone.

Grabbing the pliers, I exit the closet.

The second I step outside, there's a round of hoots and hollers as the team cheers.

Well, shit…

CHAPTER
SEVENTEEN

PENELOPE

The drive home from the kennel is a complete blur. My mind races in an attempt to make sense of my choices over the past hour. Seriously, what was I thinking?

Take your hair down.

Tell me to take off your shirt.

Tell me to take off your bra.

His words echo in my mind.

How about no, Dreven! We're in a freaking closet with everyone we work with right outside these doors!

"No.

"No.

"No.

"No."

I say the word over and over in a variety of voices. It's such a simple word, yet it escapes me when I'm near Gunner.

I'm supposed to hate the guy, not fit in a mind-blowing quickie between screwing in light bulbs. *In a closet. At work.* Wouldn't want to leave those two details out. They seem awfully important to my insanity plea, which, let's face it, is all I have to go on at the moment.

After parking my car in the drive, I run up to my front door, let myself inside, and make a beeline for my bed, where I hide beneath my covers. Maybe if I stay here long enough, I'll eventually wake up to discover this was all a very bad dream.

At this moment, I hate myself. I truly do. I've never been the girl to hide and wallow in self-pity. My life has not been easy—says the daughter of the town alcoholic, but I've always held my head high. Always.

More than anything, I'm embarrassed that I allowed Gunner to make me so weak.

Knocks sound on my door, and I ignore them.

"Go the fuck away!" I scream into my pillow.

The intrusive sound continues until, eventually, it stops. Relief doesn't find me because in a few seconds, my front door opens, and seconds after that, Iris walks into my room, holding a key in her hand.

"I found your spare key. Hope you don't mind." Her voice is entirely too chipper.

I sigh. "So I suppose everyone knows, then?" *Mental note: Kick Bash's ass.*

"Not everyone."

I sit up and lean my back against my headboard. "Great." This position and the little stretch my pants provide make me very uncomfortable. If I'm going to be talking about feelings and crap—which Iris will insist on—I need to change. Scooting off my bed, I remove my shirt and grab an oversized T-shirt.

"I knew something was there." My back is to Iris as I pull on a pair of yoga pants, but I'm sure she's grinning from ear to ear. I can hear it in her voice.

Tugging the clip from my hair, I sigh as my hair falls loose and weigh my options. I could force Iris to leave me to wallow, or I could talk to her. Both sound awful. Everything about today is complete shit.

"What do you want?" I ask.

Iris stands from my bed and steps toward me, her arms extended. "Come here."

Squinting, I eye her arms. "What are you doing?"

"I'm giving you a hug." She tilts her head to the side.

"I don't want a hug."

"As your best friend, I know when you need a hug."

I scoff. "You're not my best friend, and I don't need a hug."

She grins and steps closer. "Not only am I your best friend but I might also be your only friend."

I shake my head. "That's not true. I have lots of friends."

"Who you like?" She raises a brow.

"Well, no. But that's not a qualification for friendship."

"Come here, Pen." She closes the gap between us and wraps her arms around me. My whole body stiffens, and my arms go stiff at my sides. "Hug me back," she says, her voice soft.

The movement feels weird, but I circle my arms around her until I'm squeezing her as much as she's squeezing me. And then I'm crying. Full-on crocodile tears stream down my face as I rest against her shoulder. The embrace pulls me into this space where I'm loved and safe…and vulnerable. It's equally terrifying and comforting at the same time.

After a few minutes of snotting all over Iris's shoulder, my tears abate, and I step away.

"Let's go sit down." She heads toward the living room. "Do you want anything to drink?"

"Water is fine." I plop down onto the sofa and wrap the throw blanket around me.

Iris comes out of the kitchen with two glasses of

water and hands me one. "Tell me everything and start with the truth about Vancouver." She takes a seat in the oversized chair opposite me, placing her glass of water on the side table.

At this point, I've messed things up so much that the truth couldn't possibly make anything worse. So I tell her. I go over every emotion I felt as the events in Vancouver unfolded. I don't give her specific details about the actual sex, but I do mention frequency and the insane chemistry. I explain how it was supposed to be nothing more than a three-night fling born out of boredom.

"And I left Vancouver in the past, I did. But today in the closet, he was close, and I could tell he wanted me. That combination made me feel insane as if I had no choice. I wasn't thinking straight. I was blind to all logic and reason and only wanted him. It makes no sense because it's not me. Whoever was in that closet wasn't me, and now I don't know what will happen with the team and my job. I've screwed everything up." I suck in a breath as a new round of tears threaten to fall.

She holds her palms out to me. "First, take a deep breath. Your job will be fine. Sure, some of the guys know, but…"

Panic fills me. "But what?"

She chews on her bottom lip and lifts her eyebrows.

"Let's just say I've never seen Gunner so mad. It looked like he wanted to murder Bash. He made it very clear that if anyone said a word about you, he'd make sure they never played hockey again."

My mouth falls open. "Like he's going to break their legs or get them kicked off the team?"

Iris shrugs. "I have no idea, but I can guarantee no one is going to try to find out."

"Really?" I question, still shocked by it all.

Iris shakes her head and grins. "It's clear that you're both into one another."

"No, we're not."

"You're so into him, and from the way he just had to have you in the closet and how he defended you... he feels the same. Those kinds of emotions aren't something you feel with a booty call or a one-night stand. That's the real deal type. Like in Barbados when Cade and I did it in the bathroom by the pool and in the pool while Beckett was going on about rum. When the connection is that intense, it's love."

I bring my fingers to my temples and rub circles against my skin. "First of all, in case I wasn't clear before... I'm a hundred percent cool with never hearing another you and Cade Barbados sex story for as long as I live. Second, there is no way in hell that Gunner and I share anything resembling love. It's lust." I throw my hands up. "It has to be. For some reason, we share insane sexual chemistry, and that's all it is."

"No, it's not. You don't have to believe me now, but you'll see. The attraction you have isn't just about sex."

I jump up from the sofa and start pacing the living room floor. "How could it not be? I can't stand the guy. He's literally the bane of my existence. A hothead who makes my life so much harder."

She shrugs. "You can't choose who you love, Pen. When it's there, it's there. I think you and Gunner are very similar actually."

"Once again." I try to remain calm. "I do not love him. And how in the hell are we similar? We couldn't be more different."

"Well, you know what they say—opposites attract."

I huff out a laugh. "You know, you don't have to give advice, especially when everything that comes out of your mouth is contradictory. First, you say that we're similar, and then you say that we're opposites of one another. My head is already a complete mess without trying to connect the dots of your unsolicited logic."

"You can be both." She chuckles. "In some ways, yeah, sure, you're very different. But in others, you're the same."

I dip my chin in an exaggerated nod. "Oh… now it makes complete sense. Ugh. This is not helping."

"It's hard to explain because you're both such a closed book that I don't know what it is for sure. But you have obvious differences that everyone can see, right? That's the opposites part. However, you're both very private, quiet, standoffish, and broody. And I don't know for sure, but I feel that you're both that way for a reason, and maybe the reasons are related like you share a similar experience that made you jaded. Has he talked to you about his past?"

"No. Why would he?"

"Have you told him anything about yours?"

I pin her with a stare. "Is that a serious question?"

She grins. "Maybe you two should talk and get to know one another. Discover why you have such a connection. I'm telling you, your feelings aren't going to go away."

"My feelings," I scoff. "You know, you're really annoying. If you weren't my best friend, I'd hate you."

She throws her head back in laughter. "Ha! Told ya. I knew I was your best friend."

"Listen, I don't have feelings for Gunner. I have lust, and believe me, that will go away. Sure, he's good in that department, but that is where my attraction to him ends. I can get my needs met some other way. I'll hook up with someone else or do it myself."

"No vibrator is going to satisfy you like Gunner does, babe. Sorry to break it to you."

I shake my head. "I made a huge mistake. I can't figure out why I did it, but I'm telling you right now that I will never sleep with Gunner again."

"Is that so?" His deep voice startles me, causing me to yelp. Looking behind me, I find him leaning up against the threshold to the living room. He looks at Iris. "Leave." And as if he realizes what a dick he sounds like, he throws in a short, "Please," after a beat.

Iris jumps up from the chair and hurries out of the room, throwing a quick, "Bye, bestie! Have fun!" over her shoulder as she exits.

What a traitor.

CHAPTER **EIGHTEEN**

GUNNER

I can tell she's been crying, and I'd be lying if I said that didn't twist my insides into knots. Penny is one of the strongest women I know, and while I don't entirely understand it, her appearance and reputation are very important to her. She always comes off as completely in control, and losing ourselves to our desires in a closet during a work function is hardly in control.

She wraps her arms across her front, each hand clutching the opposite arm as if she's holding herself together. "What are you doing here?" she questions before releasing a long, low sigh.

"I came to see you."

"Why?"

I drag my fingers through my hair and blow out a breath of air. "Fuck if I know."

It's humorous, really, how two people with very little emotional maturity can fall for one another. I don't know much, but it's clear that we're both royally screwed up when it comes to intimacy and relationships.

Her posture sags before she gives a defeated shake of her head and slumps down onto the sofa.

"I guess I wanted to see you." I lean against a wall, opposite the sofa. "A few of the guys know, but I guarantee they won't speak of it again. Your job is safe, and your reputation is fine."

She snorts. "My reputation is so not fine. No...that's pretty much shot."

"You're worried about being judged by a handful of hockey players? You've worked with us. We have no room to judge you. Why does it matter what anyone thinks, anyway?"

"I don't know. It just does." She shakes her head.

As I take her in now, the realization of my feelings hits hard. I'm obsessed with this woman. That reality is undeniable. It's more than being insanely attracted to her. It's as if we have this invisible connection, a pull toward one another that's always been there. Unhealed traumas morphed this unearthly pull into something else—hatred or, at the very least, annoyance. Yet I can no longer stick my head in the sand and pretend that's all it is. The pair of us is broken. There's no question about that. Yet I can't help but feel that together, maybe we can be whole.

These ideas in my head sound cheesy even to me. Perhaps I'll never have the courage to voice them out loud, but I feel them, nonetheless, and something inside me demands that I honor them.

I approach the sofa and extend my hand. "Come here."

Her brows furrow as her big brown eyes dart from my hand to my face with uncertainty.

"I don't bite."

She forces a laugh. "I doubt that." But she takes my hand, and I pull her up.

I thread my fingers through her thick curls, tilting her face toward mine. "I want you... and not in the way I've had you but in all the ways I haven't."

Pulling her head back slightly, she swallows hard. "What do you...?" Her words are soft as her voice trails off.

Lifting my shoulders, I shrug. "I'm not sure what that entails, I only know that I lied to you. I think about Vancouver all the fucking time. Yet the truth is, I thought about you long before then. I'm not good at this. I have no idea where to start or what to do, but I know I want you."

Dead. Fucking. Silence.

If she wasn't blinking, I'd question whether she was still breathing. My heart races inside my chest. I pull my hands from her hair and drop them at my sides. My breath is shallow, and my mind becomes fuzzy. I'm stuck in this place of uncertainty. Is this a rejection?

Finally, she dips her chin in a nod and says, "Okay."

"Okay?"

The corners of her mouth tilt up in a slight grin. "I think it's crazy. We're probably the two people least equipped to be in a relationship..." She quirks a brow. "You are asking me to be in a relationship, right?"

"I guess."

"You guess?" she scoffs. "This is serious, Gunner. You need to know."

I throw my hands up. "Cut me some slack, Penny. I've never done this. I don't do labels. All I know is I want you."

"Only me?"

"Only you."

"Okay."

"Okay?" We've regressed to speaking like cave people. At this point, I think it'd be more clear if I just threw her ass over my shoulder, took her to the bedroom, and sealed the deal. This back-and-forth is giving me a headache. "So... what do we do now?"

After a beat, she says, "Let's nap."

"Nap?"

"It's been an exhausting month." She takes my hand and leads me to her bedroom. "I'm emotionally spent. Aren't you?"

"Uh, yeah, okay." Maybe nap is code for the fun stuff. Regardless, I'm in.

Penny pulls back the covers and climbs onto her bed, leaving a space for me behind her. She faces away from me. With the blanket on us, I lie against her back, wrapping my arm around her waist. We lie in this position, and I wait, allowing her to take the lead. Only, after a few minutes, her breathing shallows, and I realize that nap wasn't code for anything.

This is new.

I can't say I hate it.

Penny's body is warm against mine. The soft rise and fall of her chest creates a soothing cadence. The scent of her shampoo, a sultry fruity mixture, wafts through the air along with hints of cinnamon coming from somewhere else in the room. It's all—pleasant and strange.

Long minutes are spent trying to figure it all out and rationalize the situation, but eventually I realize that it doesn't matter. I'm here. With her. Labels, midday naps, and spooning aside—that feels right.

The dream was forgotten as soon as my mind awakened, but it was a good one, and my sense of happiness remains. It's a stark contrast to the night-mares that usually plague my sleep. Sweet and spicy hit my senses, and my eyelids pop open.

Penny is turned toward me now, awake and staring directly at me. "That was a good nap, huh?"

"Uh, yeah." I stretch my arms out over my head and move my neck to the side. The familiar cracks of my spine sound.

"Are you still in the same place you were before we fell asleep?" She keeps her voice steady. A bit of work Penny comes through, and I know she's putting on some of her armor to ward off disappointment.

I swipe a lock of her hair behind her ear. It's possibly the first time I've ever completed that motion with a woman in my life, and it's oddly satisfying. "If you're referring to the place where I only want to be with you. Then yes."

She smiles, a genuine, beautiful smile. "Good. I was thinking we should take a hot bath, get comfy clothes on, order takeout, and talk."

"Is any of that code for sex? I thought maybe napping was code for sex, but I was wrong about that.

So just so I know what to expect… what should I expect?"

"You can pretty much take what I say at face value."

"So we're together, alone, and in an actual decent bed, but there will be no sex?"

She nods. "Correct."

"I'm liking this dating stuff already."

She chuckles. "Who knew Gunner Dreven could make a joke."

"That wasn't a joke," I deadpan, which elicits another laugh from Penny.

"I just think we should get to know each other. We already know that we have insane chemistry in the sex department. We'll have no problems there. But neither of us are relationship people, and if we're really going to do this, we should see if we actually like each other or are compatible in other ways. If we don't, we're just wasting our time."

"Sex with you is never a waste of time."

"Yeah, but a relationship would be. Being together impacts a lot of things for us. It's going to change the dynamic at work. We need to make sure that we really want to do this… whatever this is."`

"Work won't change. I'll do my thing, and you'll do yours, as always. I am nothing like Beckett or Cade, for that matter." I think of my teammates, the two starting forwards, and how they turned into lovesick saps following their girls around. They practically have hearts pop out of their eyes when they see their wives. "I don't do relationships, let alone ones with PDA at work."

"Works for me," she says.

"Good. I want to keep us between us, if that makes sense?"

She pulls her bottom lip into her mouth, and it takes all my willpower not to lean in for a kiss. "You want to keep the fact that we're seeing one another a secret?"

"No." I place my hand on her hip. "It's not that. I don't care if people know. But when we're together, I want it to be just us without all the outside noise."

She raises a brow. "That only works if you can refrain from random quickies in the storage closet."

"I have control."

"Well, you didn't show any today."

"I showed as much as you did."

She puckers her lips. "That's fair." Backing away, she climbs out of the other side of the bed and makes her way to the connected bathroom. "I'm going to run a bath. You can join me if you want."

I don't remember a time when I chose a bath over a shower in my adult life, but if it involves a naked Penny, I'm in.

CHAPTER
NINETEEN

PENNY

My slick body lies atop Gunner's, limp and buzzing with the afterglow of satisfaction. The jets from the Jacuzzi tub push bubbles of water across my skin as I breathe in the steamy air.

So much for my no-sex declaration.

However, did I think that bathing with Gunner would lead to another mind-blowing orgasm? I'd be lying if I said no. Apparently, the two of us will never not take advantage of being naked together.

I was serious about wanting to talk and getting to know one another. But a little romp in the tub never hurt anyone. Now that it's out of our system, we can go back to the regularly scheduled program, which, when I stop to truly think about it, is insane. We're going to get to know each other…Gunner and me… and talk about our relationship.

So strange.

I am naked in the tub in my house, straddling the Crane's goalie, who, up to a month ago, I couldn't stand. The two of us have no business partaking in anything labeled "a relationship," yet here we are. Granted, we're only a few hours in, so the jury is still out. This could all end in an epic disaster, but something inside me needs to find out.

Propping myself up, I splay my palm across his chest and run it across his wet skin. The guy is an Adonis; every inch of his body is sculpted to perfection. Some of the more outgoing guys on the team have the hot guy reputation, but I don't find any of them more attractive than Gunner. I tilt my face up, resting my chin on his chest as I take him in. His dark black hair is disheveled, the short cut just long enough to allow chunks to fall to the side. A sexy five-o'clock shadow covers his face. His eyes, a deep brown with dark lashes, hold a kindness that I don't think many people see. Truthfully, I've never looked at his eyes long enough to see it myself.

He is one big, beautiful beast of a man. And he's… mine?

My reality has been turned upside down over the past month. I was so sure about things that I now realize I got wrong. I haven't quite figured Gunner out, but he's not the man I thought he was. He's so much more than I gave him credit for. He came here inviting me into his life to know him in a way that I don't think many do.

My steel heart is starting to feel things I haven't felt in a long time. It's scary, and I'm questioning myself. It's too soon to trust my feelings. Though, part of me wants to. I yearn to dive in headfirst, heart open to experience a love like I've never known.

Maybe.

But what if I'm wrong? What if this isn't real?

I've spent my life building a fort around my heart to protect myself. I've never been against love, but I won't be vulnerable. In my earliest memories, it was me against the world. I've always been the only one who I could count on, and that hasn't changed. Gushy fantasies of lifelong orgasms and a dreamy alpha male to love me for all eternity are alluring, but the fact remains, at the end of the day, there's only me. I'm willing to see where this goes, but the protections stay in place. They have to.

"What's going on in that head of yours?" Gunner's deep voice breaks my train of thought.

"Just thinking we should probably get out."

"Sure because we have all that talking to do." He sounds less than amused.

I push myself up from his slick body. Standing, I grab a towel, wrap it around my body, and step out. "Don't sound too excited." I offer him a towel.

"I'm excited about food." He steps out of the tub. "I'm starving."

With another towel, I bend at the waist and scrunch the water from my hair. I catch Gunner eyeing me with a look of fascination. The guy definitely has something for my hair. "I'm starving, too. What about Thai?"

"I could do Thai. Have you tried All that Thai? They have the best…"

"Drunken noodles," we say in unison.

I chuckle. "It's definitely a drunken noodle kind of night."

An hour later, we're sitting on my oversized sofa, each at the opposite end with our Thai noodles. I'm sporting oversized sweatpants and a baggy T-shirt, while Gunner wears the jeans and T-shirt he came in. Our get-to-know-you session has resulted in eye-opening revelations. For instance, I now know that Gunner loves playing hockey and Thai food. While he's learned that I have a love/hate relationship with my job, and not only do I love Thai food but I'm also a coffee addict.

I mean, the deep levels of vulnerability we've experienced here are shattering.

Slurping my final noodle into my mouth, I set the empty plastic to-go container on the coffee table behind me. "Don't you wish there was a way to fast-forward through the awful get-to-know-you dates? I dread them, and in the past, they've been a waste of time anyway. Most guys don't stick around very long. So why go through all the questions to begin with. You know?"

"Why don't most guys stick around?"

"Because I don't want them to."

He nods as if that's all the explanation he needs. "I've never made it to the get-to-know-you dates in a relationship."

My brows raise. "Really?"

"Really."

"And why is that?"

"Because I don't date."

"But you want to date me?"

"Yeah."

The one word makes my heart twist. "You're thirty-three. Why haven't you had a serious relationship before now?"

He sets his take-out container down and releases a

long sigh. I can see him weighing his options. To share or not to share. This is a make-or-break moment in this potential relationship. "Until recently, I've never been in the presence of a healthy relationship. I grew up surrounded by toxic ones, and I've never wanted that in my life."

"Your parents?"

He shakes his head. Looking down, he's quiet for a minute, clearly deciding how much to share with me. I can tell he's never gotten to this part of a relationship before. He clears his throat and raises his gaze to meet mine. "I never knew my dad. It was always only ever my mom and the piece of trash she was dating at the moment."

"And I'm guessing there was a lot of trash?"

He nods slowly, a frown on his face. "Tons."

"I didn't know my dad either, and my mom was the town drunk. I basically raised myself so there wouldn't be any red flags that would cause concern and get me taken away from her." It's not like me to be this open, but I feel surprisingly comfortable with Gunner. Not to mention, I'm the one who initiated this whole get-to-know-each-other conversation. If I want him to be open and honest, I have to do the same.

"That's why you are the way you are," he states.

"Meaning?"

"You present this badass version of yourself, prim

and proper, and always in control with your boring pantsuits and pulled-back twist without a hair out of place. You need to control the narrative the way you did growing up."

"I suppose so."

"It must be extremely frustrating trying to control us heathens." A small smile finds his lips.

I force out a dry chuckle. "You have no idea."

"So… your mom now? Is she better?" His voice holds a sweet tone of concern.

I shrug. "She's six feet under, so… I don't know if that's better than living the way she was or not."

"I'm sorry."

"Yeah, well… one can't chug vodka like water for thirty years and think they'll live a long life."

"So that's why I never see you drink."

"Partly. I don't have anything against casual drinking. I know that's the way of the world. But they say alcoholism is hereditary, and I've never wanted to push my luck. Plus, the thought of being out of control is something I can't fathom. Not to mention, you only see me at work functions, and I'd never drink on the job anyway. But no, I'm not a big drinker."

"Yeah, me either," he says.

I quirk my brow with a scoff. "Yeah, right. You always have a beer in your hand at the bars after a game."

"True. I'll have a beer or two, but you've never seen me drunk because I never am. I, too, like to be in control."

Thinking back to the years I've known Gunner, I can't remember a time when he was obviously drunk. He's always the same, a grumpy guy of few words. I'd assumed he was the same way when drinking. His statement is hard to believe. It shatters years of preconceived notions, but I have no evidence to the contrary. It's not that I wouldn't date someone who drank. I know that people can get tipsy and have fun without having a problem. However, it's oddly another thing we have in common.

I'm not quite sure if I find our many similarities comforting or unsettling. Because of his past, he can see into me in a way that no one ever has. He understands. We've barely gotten to know each other, and already, I feel as if there's no hiding.

Speaking of parallels, I ask, "How about your mom? Has she gotten better choosing a man?"

Gunner's entire frame goes stiff, and my heart beats rapidly in my chest. The air in the room has shifted. Gunner stands and collects the take-out containers.

"She's dead." His voice is low and firm with his response. It's only two words, but they carry a finality, and I'm well aware that our getting-to-know-you session is over.

CHAPTER
TWENTY

GUNNER

I dig my hand into the plastic bag Sebastian handed me, pull out a fresh scone, and take a bite.

"Motherfucker, Bash," I say through a mouthful of heavenly goodness. "We're going to have to think of a new nickname for you because you can make way more than cookies."

"It's good, right?" He grins.

"Fuck, yeah. I always thought scones were dry. This isn't dry at all." I take another bite.

"Well, the key to making sure it doesn't come out dry is to…"

I hold up a hand, halting what was sure to be a very long-winded explanation on how to make the perfect scone. "Dude, you know I'm never going to make these myself. Don't waste your baking knowledge on me. Are they cinnamon?"

"Yeah, apple cinnamon."

"These would be good with coffee," I say, though I myself am not a coffee fan. Yet I know a sassy redhead who would love these with her coffee. I make a mental note to save her a couple even though I could easily devour this entire bag.

As if he can read my mind, Bash says, "Penny will love them."

I nod.

Not taking the hint, he continues, "So you and Penny, huh?"

If he were anyone else, I might tell him to shut his mouth in a non-polite way, but it's not easy to be a dick to Sebastian Calloway. At twenty-four years old, he's the youngest on the team, and he embodies the baby brother role. He looks younger than his age with his floppy sandy-blond hair, big blue eyes, and dimple. Plus, he just seems young and innocent. I've seen him with some puck bunnies, so I know he's anything but innocent, yet I can't help but feel protective over him.

I toss the remainder of the ziplock bag of scones on the top of my clothes in my duffel, careful not to squish them before I zip up my gym bag. I got my lifting in early today, and now that practice is finished, I have a few hours before Penny leaves work. Since I've been staying at her place, I'm going to run home and grab some more clothes before she gets off.

"How's that going? You guys hitting it off?" Bash asks.

I raise a brow. "How about we talk about whoever you've been secretly texting over the past six months? You know, the one who makes you smile like a schoolboy when you text her? We should take a deep dive into that conversation."

Bash's eyes go wide. "Oh, gotcha. Penny questions are off-limits. Got it. See you later, Gun." Turning on his heel, he hikes up his gym bag and heads for the door.

I chuckle. "Thanks for the scones, Cookie."

He waves without turning back.

The truth is, I don't care who Bash is seeing. He has his right to privacy. If anyone gets that, I do. But that doesn't mean I don't know he's secretly talking to someone. The kid is constantly on his phone, though he's never mentioned a word about the person he's texting, which is different for him because I usually can't get the kid to shut up. He's not one to be hush-hush about anything. It's clear he doesn't want to talk about his current relationship or whatever it is with the team, just as I don't. Only with me, it's impossible to date Penny in complete secrecy, given we work together. However, I'll be damned if I'm going to participate in conversations about my dating life.

After a trip home to grab more clothes and run a few errands, I head over to Penny's place, and thankfully, she's home.

I knock a couple of times on the front door.

She swings the door open. "Hey, I told you that you don't have to knock. Just come in." She steps to the side, inviting me in.

"Yeah, I know, but that feels weird." And it does. As much fun as I'm having with Penny, this whole dating scene is still very new, and just walking into someone's home feels strange.

Penny scrunches her wet hair with a towel. She wears a baggy T-shirt and cotton shorts. Her makeup-free face reminds me of our time in Vancouver. Something about Penny in this state, without her power suit, hairdo, and done-up face, is so attractive to me.

"You showered without me." I follow her into the living room.

She chuckles. "Yeah, and it was nice. I actually got to shave my legs. When you're in there, we get distracted."

"I like getting distracted."

"Yeah, our distractions are pretty nice." She hangs the towel on the back of the chair and grabs the remote from the side table before plopping on the sofa. She taps the spot next to her.

"One second. Let me put this away." I hold up my duffel. I grab her damp towel from the chair as I make my way to the bedroom. I hang her towel on the towel bar in the bathroom and retrieve the bag of scones before leaving my bag beside the bed and returning to the living room.

I groan when I see the TV. "Again? Do you watch anything else?"

"No. Why would I? *Friends* is the best."

"You've seen all the episodes a hundred times. Don't you get tired of them?"

She shakes her head. "Nope. Love 'em."

I hold up the clear plastic bag. "Bash made cinnamon scones. They'd be great with coffee. Want them now or tomorrow with your coffee?"

She claps her hands. "Ooh, one now and the rest later."

I toss her a scone and put the rest on the kitchen counter. "This is amazing. Seriously, are we sure that kid went into the right field?"

Sebastian is only three years younger than Penny, but she even refers to him as a kid. "Yeah, he's quite the baker, but he's a damn good center, too." As the rookie on the team, it's not common to be a starter, but

Bash has been a starter since his first day on the team. He's that good.

"I think he was Betty Crocker in his former life," she says.

I join Penny on the sofa. "Is Betty Crocker a real person? I thought it was just the name of a cookbook."

"I don't know." Penny shrugs, picking up her phone. "Ah, Google says that Betty Crocker is a brand, but there is a real woman behind the brand named Marjorie Child Husted. Weird. I always thought the name of the woman behind Betty Crocker was Betty Crocker."

"Well, is this Marjorie lady still alive?"

"No, she died in 1986."

"Well then I suppose Bash could be Marjorie reincarnated."

"Or some fancy pastry chef that we don't know about." She plops the last bite of the scone in her mouth.

I circle my arm around Penny's shoulders. "I guess we'll never know, just as we'll never know if Ross and Rachel end up together. These two have more back-and-forth than anyone should. Watch her end up with someone else, like Chandler," I tease.

Penny rears back, her brows furrowed. "Wait, you really don't know who Rachel or Chandler end up with?"

I chuckle. "No, why would I? I told you I've never watched the show."

"I know but even people who haven't *watched* the show have watched the show. You know? Everyone has seen bits and pieces of it throughout the years when it's playing in hotels or in the background somewhere."

"I really haven't seen any episodes besides the ones I've watched with you, so I don't know how it all ends."

"Oh my gosh. We have to start from the beginning so you can get the whole experience."

I shake my head. "No, we really don't. It's okay. I'm fine with a limited experience."

She holds the remote toward the TV and goes to the menu. "No, if you saw it from the beginning, then you'd get the hype."

"Pen...I really don't..." I say as Penny clicks on season one, episode one. "Okaay, we're starting at the beginning."

She grins wide. "You are going to love it. Next, I'll get you to love coffee."

"Neither of those things are happening."

"Maybe coffee is an acquired taste, but everyone loves *Friends*."

"I don't think that's true, Pen."

She pauses the show and puckers her lips. "Oooh,

what should we order? We need something good to start our marathon. Chinese?"

"That works for me. Make sure to order extra crab rangoons."

"Done." She nods, tapping away on her phone to create an online order for the local Chinese restaurant. "I hope Willa is delivering tonight. She never forgets any of the sauces."

I chuckle. Penny is a condiment girl. While she orders, I grab my phone and Venmo her some money, which she'll complain about later, but my date isn't paying for my dinner.

"They must be busy tonight. Delivery is in over an hour." She unpauses the show. "That gives us like three episodes."

"Is this what dating couples do? Watch *Friends* and eat takeout?"

"I have no idea. This is all a first for me, too. But, this is what we're going to do," she says with sass.

"Oh really?"

"Really."

"I know something else this dating couple is going to do."

She pins me with a stare. "We have food coming."

"In an hour. That gives us plenty of time."

Leaning in, I pepper kisses over her neck, and she releases a content sigh. I pull her earlobe into my mouth, and she hums in pleasure. I continue to trail kisses across her skin. When she lifts her arm, remote in hand, and clicks the TV off, I know I've won.

"Good choice." I take hold of her waist and lift her on top of me so she's straddling my legs.

"It wasn't much of a choice," she says as I take hold of the bottom of her T-shirt and pull it over her head.

"No, it really wasn't."

I flick her nipple with my tongue. "Now, this is what dating couples do."

She giggles. "Less talking, more action. Make me feel good."

"Now that I can do."

CHAPTER
TWENTY-ONE

PENNY

My calendar obsession is no joke. I seriously don't know how I'd live without them. I scan the one on the screen in front of me and it's color-coded perfection. My life and the entirety of the Crane Organization are planned down to the minute in stunning, organized detail. This calendar syncs with my phone, and just because I'm a little crazy, I write it all down in my paper day planner that is stored in my purse. Digital calendars have their place, for sure. However, nothing is more satisfying than crossing off to-do list items on paper.

There's a knock on my office door. "Come in."

The team doctor and our starting forward's wife, Elena, walks into the room. I like Elena. She's a strong woman with a lot of integrity. Unlike my relationship with Iris, the one I have with Elena has always been professional. We haven't crossed into an out-of-work friendship. Much like me, Elena focuses on work when she's here and leaves when she's done. She's not the Chatty Cathy that her sister-in-law Iris is, and I respect that. In fact, the sole reason Iris and I are as close as we are has everything to do with her and nothing to do with me.

"Hi, Penelope. I know there is a fan meet and greet after the game tonight, and I was wondering if I could hold Mr. Lewis back. His hamstring has been a little sore, and I want to make sure he gets in his stretching to keep him in top shape with the playoffs next month. Can't risk any injuries," she says.

"Oh, absolutely. No problem. I didn't advertise which players would be there so we could use who was available. With these guys, you never know. So Jaden is all yours."

"Great. Thanks so much."

"How are you feeling?"

She puts her hand on her very large belly. "Tired." She gives a half chuckle, half sigh. "Pregnant at forty is not for the weak. I just hope the little one holds out until his or her daddy is done for the season."

Taking her in now, I find it hard to believe she still has two months of pregnancy left. She looks like she could pop at any moment. "It's going to be close. I really think the guys have a shot of getting to the cup finals this year."

"I know." She nods. "And I truly hope they do. It's going to be interesting. I just don't want Beckett to miss the birth if he's away at a road game. I won't be able to travel with him toward the end."

"Yeah, that's tough. Well, hopefully, it all works out."

She smiles. "Yes. I'm hoping so. Anyway, thanks again."

"No problem."

Elena exits my office as a notification for a new email pops up. It's a project request for our charity Cranes Cares. My calendar is booked for the afternoon, but I make myself a note to look into the submission tomorrow.

"Hey!" Iris singsongs, closing the door to my office behind her.

I raise a brow, knowing that 'hey' is not work-related. "Yes?"

"Just checking in." She clasps her hands in front of her and takes a seat in the chair facing my desk.

"On?"

"Just life." She shrugs.

"The meet and greet all set?"

She bobs her head. "Yep, my to-do list is done. All

the i's and t's are crossed. So I thought I'd touch base with my friend Penny. I saw you and Gunner arrive together this morning. Things are getting serious?"

"It's more efficient. Doesn't make sense to drive two cars." My response is met with an expectant stare that makes me grin. I roll my eyes and huff out a laugh. "What do you want to know?"

She leans forward and grasps the arms of the chair. "Uh, everything. I've barely seen or spoken to you since this new development in your love life. You can't leave your bestie hanging like that."

"I already told you… we're dating."

She pouts her lips and shoots me a glare. "Duh. I need details."

"Like?"

"You are so bad at this." She tosses her head back in a laugh. "How's it going? What do you guys do every night? Is he different with you, or does he only communicate in grunts?"

I smile. "He's different. I mean, he's not talking my ear off or anything, but we talk. We hang out, watch TV, order dinner, have sex, and go to bed."

"And the sex is good?"

I sigh, leaning back in my chair. "Yeah. It's pretty damn good."

"Like how good?"

"The best I've had."

She slaps her hand on my desk. "I knew it. You two are endgame."

My brows furrow. "Stop. It's way too soon to know that."

"Nuh-uh. It's not. I can tell. It was the same with Cade and me. Once we got together, we had this explosive chemistry. That only happens, to that degree, with your person. It makes sense. When you stop to think about it, you two are really alike."

"True. We are, and that kind of scares me. I thought the relationships that work are between people who are different, the whole opposites attract saying... like Beckett and Elena."

"There is no tried-and-tested rule. It just depends on the people. I don't know...I get this feeling that you and Gunner are made for each other."

"Well, it's a little soon for all that anyway."

She shrugs. "Eh, when you know, you know. You know?"

I chuckle. "I don't know, and neither do you. Are you sure you don't have any work to do?" I reach for my day planner.

Iris bolts up from the chair and holds out her hands, palms toward me. "I'll find something. No need to rifle through that thing."

"For a lawyer, you're quite gabby. You know?"

"Have you ever met a lawyer? We're all gabby. We

literally talk for a living. And...was. I was a lawyer. Now, I plan parties, hang out with you, and watch my hubby play hockey. This life is totally me."

"Good. I'm glad you're happy."

She completes a half twirl and reaches for my office door. "And I'm glad you're happy. I can't wait to hear more. You need to practice your gossip delivery. It's a little bland."

I tear my gaze away from my computer and direct it to Iris. "I'll work on it."

"That's all I ask." She shrugs. "Now, if you'll excuse me, I'm going to steal my hubby away before he dresses for the game and sneak in a little closet make-out session or something." She winks. "You know? You should try it."

"Go away. We don't do that."

"That's not what I heard," she teases before hurrying out of my office.

The Crane boys pulled out a three-to-one win against Toronto. It was a fun game to watch. I sat next to Iris and her family. They were all sporting number ten jerseys for Cade or eighteen for Beckett, while I was wearing the pantsuit I wore to work this morning. I wonder if I'll ever be in a place where I'll wear jeans and Dreven's number? It doesn't seem like something I'd do.

Just as Iris said it would, the meet and greet went off without a hitch. Both the fans and players were ecstatic after the win. The arena has cleared of fans, and most everyone has left.

Gunner, freshly showered and wearing jeans and a black T-shirt that hugs his biceps, steps out of the locker room with his duffel bag in hand.

"Good game." I give him a smile.

He smacks me on the ass. "Thanks. Let's get out of here."

"Everyone's heading to the bar. Did you want to meet up?"

"Nah. Not in the mood tonight. Let's just head back to your place."

I bite my bottom lip in thought.

Gunner releases a deep chuckle beside me. "Trust me. Grown-ass men can handle a night out without you."

"Are we sure, though? You're all nothing but troublemakers. What if something goes wrong, and I'm not there to smooth it out?"

"They'll manage. Has anyone ever told you that you're a control freak?" he opens the door to the car garage, and I pass him, exiting the building.

I shoot him a mock glare. "Maybe once or twice."

This causes a smile to form on his face. Grumpy and broody Gunner is one attractive man, but happy Gunner is hot as hell. I love making him smile.

"You know it's not your job to follow us to the bars." He opens the passenger side door, and I slide in.

I wait until he's walked around the vehicle and slid into the driver's seat to answer. "I know, but being there when a mess happens so I can immediately do damage control makes my life a lot easier."

He backs out of the space and pulls out onto the road. "You don't have much faith in us, do you?"

I scoff.

"Look on the bright side. I won't be there. So less likely to be issues."

"True."

Gunner smiles again, and I have to stop myself from sighing. He's beautiful.

I ask some questions about the game, and it gets him talking. He's definitely not much of a conversationalist, but he gets going when he's chatting about a game.

Gunner's mouth is on mine the second my front door closes behind us. God, this man can kiss. "I've been waiting to do that all night," he says between kisses.

"Oh yeah?" My lips grin against his.

"Oh yeah."

With my back up against the door, Gunner cups my chin, directing my mouth exactly where he wants it to go. He releases an anguished moan into my mouth as his tongue dances with mine. His kisses are addictive. I circle my arms around his tight back muscles and pull him into me, wanting to feel his strong body against mine.

He pulls away, panting, and retrieves something from his discarded duffel bag on the floor. Then he pushes a piece of clothing into my hands, and his words come out gravelly and needy. "Go put this on. I want to fuck you in nothing but this."

I don't question the demand. I slip past him and into my room, where I quickly remove my clothing. It takes my lust-filled brain a second to realize that the item in my hand is his jersey. I hold the navy blue Crane's jersey with the white number twenty-nine.

Holy hell. Desire pools, and I throw his jersey over my head and pull it down over my bare skin in record time.

Gunner lumbers into the room, discarding his clothing as he enters. He halts and takes me in, his stare feral, and his chest heaves as he pulls in a breath. His big brown eyes take me in from my head to my toes and back again. The way he looks at me makes me feel like the most beautiful woman in the world and sends my pulse careening.

He stands naked before me, and it's clear just how much I turn him on. "Almost," he utters through pained breaths, holding my stare.

"Oh." I reach up and unclip my hair, letting it fall over my shoulders, and toss the clip to the floor.

"Fucking perfect."

He closes the distance between us and wraps his arms around me, lifting me off the ground. I circle my legs around his ass. In a few steps, he has me pinned against the wall, and he's entering me hard and fast. As he slips deep inside me, we moan in unison.

Bending his knees, he thrusts up, hitting my insides at the perfect angle. I chant my approval over and over. Sex with Gunner is always good. Sometimes he takes it slow with lots of foreplay, and other times, he gets right to the main event, and it's just as amazing. His moves are punishingly sweet, and my entire body hums as he works me higher and higher.

"Are you mine?" he groans, holding my stare.

"Yes," I pant. My body starts to tremble as the impending euphoria rises. "I'm yours."

He works his thrusts harder, and his chest glistens with sweat. "Then you better fucking show it." His words resonate but barely as I focus in on my pleasure. With a flick of his finger, he'll have me soaring, and he knows it. I want to come so bad that I'm out of my mind. "Penny..."

"I'll show it. I'll show it," I cry out as his hand slips between my legs and rubs the bundle of nerves that sends me flying.

Two orgasms later, we lie in my bed. The jersey has been tossed to the floor. I lie beside him, and our heated skin is pressed together. I trace lazy circles over his chest muscles, and his fingers trail up and down my back in a rhythmic motion as we both catch our breath.

"Does twenty-nine have a significance?" I ask before pressing my lips against his chest in a peck.

His body stiffens. "Hmm?"

"Your jersey number? A lot of the guys pick numbers that are significant to them for one reason or another. Did you... pick a meaningful number or just get assigned one?"

He pulls his arm out from behind my head and sits up. "I think we could use a shower. Yeah?"

"Gunner. My question. Are you going to answer it?"

"No." He swings his legs over the side of the bed and stands.

"Seriously?" My tone raises an octave. "It's a simple question." I scurry off the bed and follow him into the bathroom.

He turns on the water and steps into the shower, leaving me confused. "Gunner," I protest.

"Drop it, Penny. That's a story for another day."

The emotion in his voice is out of place, and if I'm not mistaken, it sounds a little like sorrow. I don't ask the question again.

Nothing about this relationship is what I would classify as normal, and for the most part, I'm okay with it. We're both on a learning curve of sorts. Yet Gunner is holding back more than me. And though I think I want to be his, I'm not. We can't belong to one another if we don't truly know one another. He needs time, and I understand that. But I can't pretend I'm not nervous. If he can't trust me enough to let me in, we have an expiration date—it's that simple.

We've barely started, yet the thought of losing him scares me. More than it probably should.

CHAPTER
TWENTY-TWO

GUNNER

This has been the longest practice of my life. It's monotonous and never-ending. I'd swear it was twice as long as normal if I wasn't watching the clock tick by on the wall.

Something is seriously wrong with me. I can't focus or think about anything other than her. Is this what being pussy-whipped feels like? I mean, I've teased many a teammate of being just that hundreds of times, but I've never experienced it myself. It's more than sex I want with Penny, though. I want it all. When I'm not with her, I'm thinking about when I will be.

I'm Penny whipped.

It's equal parts incredible and horrific at the same

time. I've never seen myself as a relationship kind of guy. Yet when I'm with her, I'm happy. Me...happy. Her presence brings a sense of calm that covers me like a blanket, and that feeling is addicting. Truthfully, it's terrifying. It's only been a month since we made things official, and I'm starting to *need* her. I don't *need* anyone. I don't want to need anyone. Yet... I want her. I'm already in deep. I play it off as if it's casual, but I can't hide from myself.

She's come into the arena a few times this morning to converse with Coach as she is now. Her form-fitting pantsuit is a deep forest green. Her pale complexion and burnt-red hair stand out in that color, making her more stunning than usual. I use all my willpower to focus on the drills at hand, but my eyes dart to where she stands. Her hair is pulled back in a twist, and my fingers tingle with the need to pull that clip off her head and run my fingers through her curly locks.

A puck whizzes by my head, hitting the net behind me.

"Dude, where are you today?" Beckett shakes his head. "You need to get your shit together. Playoffs are coming up, and we're going all the way this year," he says before retreating to the other side of the ice.

I can't even argue with him because he's right. My head isn't in this practice. It's with her, and that's a problem.

Turning my attention back to the ice where it should be, I ignore her as she retreats from the ice. I don't watch her perfectly delectable ass as she moves up the steps toward the offices. I don't imagine what it will be like to grab on to said ass, naked tonight. Not even a little bit.

By some small miracle, the longest practice in history finally ends, and we head to the showers. I take my time, knowing that Penny usually works later. Though I have been on my best behavior since we've started dating. The good deeds tour, even with the closet indiscretion, was a PR success, so maybe she won't work as late as she normally does.

The guys make plans to meet up at the Mongolian Grill tonight for dinner, but I give a couple of grunts as to why I won't be there, and they don't press me further.

I'm last to leave the locker room, and a grin surfaces when I find Penny waiting for me in the hall outside the locker room.

She quirks a brow. "And you call me a princess? What were you doing in there for so long?"

I supply a shrug, and we head out of the building together. "I'm surprised you're done so early."

"Yeah, it's nice when things are smooth sailing. Rare but nice." She nudges my side. My hand itches to grab hers, and while everyone knows we're dating, we've yet to display any PDA at work, per Penny's wishes. "What do you feel like doing for dinner? Iris says everyone is meeting up. Any interest?"

"Not really."

"Good. Me either." There's an air of relief in her voice. "Order in?"

"Sounds good."

Without discussion, we get in my car and head to her place. We've yet to stay at mine, and save for the handful of times I've stopped there to grab clothes, I haven't been there all month. There's just something about her condo that I like. It's comfortable. In comparison, mine feels cold. It's the kind of place that one who has a rotating string of women stop by for an emotionless quickie would stay, not someone in a relationship. Penny's place feels like monogamy, and I dig it.

"Do you need to stop by your place?" she asks from the passenger seat.

"Nah, I grabbed enough yesterday."

She nods. "So how was practice?"

"Very long. How was work?" I turn onto her street.

"Same. Long and uneventful. What should we order in?"

"I don't know. Whatever you want."

"We should make something," she suggests.

"Do you have ingredients?"

"No. We'd have to go to the store."

I release a sigh and pass her condo, continuing to the grocery store a few blocks past her place. I loathe going out in public. While I don't think I'm a celebrity by any means, this is Crane territory, and everyone in this area is a fan. I hate the pictures, small talk, and signatures. In my downtime, I don't want to have to deal with any of that. I just want to veg out. Going out in public makes me feel like I never leave work. I have to smile and be friendly when I don't feel like doing either. It's exhausting.

Sensing my hesitation, she says, "It will be quick. In and out. You can even stay in the car if you want."

"No, I'll go in with you."

I park the car, get out, and walk around to Penny's side. Opening her door, I extend my hand and help her out. It's an old-school gesture and doesn't seem like something I would do, but I have to admit, I love it. A few weeks ago, we arrived to work, and Penny was busy on her phone, so I went around to her door and opened it for her. The gesture felt right, and I've been doing it ever since. I have this innate desire to take care of her in every way possible.

Penny thanks me and leans her back against the car. She circles her arms around my neck and pulls me against her. Palms splayed against the car, I cage her in.

"I missed you today," she says before leaning up and pressing her lips to mine.

A feral growl sounds from the back of my throat, and I deepen the kiss. I circle one of my arms around her back and pull her against me while my other hand undoes the metal clip in her hair. My fingers thread through her hair, holding her face to mine as my mouth worships hers. My tongue circles hers as our lips fight for more. Kissing Penny is intoxicating, but it's never enough.

She cups my cheeks with her hands and pulls away panting, a smile crosses her face. "I'm guessing you missed me too?"

"Fuck yeah, I did." I'm so hard beneath my jeans as I lean into her. I know she feels it.

She scratches her manicured nails lightly against the scruff of my face. "We need to focus. What do you want to make to eat?"

"You know I'll eat anything."

"I know, but aren't you craving anything? Is there something that your mom used to make for you that sounds good?"

She hasn't brought up my mother since I told her she was dead, and I want to be angry that she is now, but I know that this talking shit is part of being in a relationship. Seeing that I'm currently obsessed with Penny, I have to play the game. Nothing about opening up comes easy, but I want Penny enough to try.

I take a second to consider her question. "Well, she used to make a killer grilled cheese and tomato soup."

"Grilled cheese and tomato soup? That's what you're craving?"

"Yeah."

"It must be a generation thing. My mom didn't cook much, but she could make a delicious grilled cheese," she says.

"Cheap white bread, processed American cheese, and generic condensed tomato soup?"

"Yep!" She grins. "The cheaper the better. Maybe it wasn't so much a generational thing but a poor thing."

"Maybe," I agree. "Regardless, it's tasty."

"It is." She pushes off from the car and threads her fingers through mine as we start for the store entrance. "I haven't had this meal in years."

"Me either."

I'm feeling good as we enter the store. She was able to pull out a piece of my past without making it a painful experience. The more time I spend with her, the more I realize that she may be the one person on this earth for me. I always thought that I was destined to live my life alone, but I'm seeing now that I don't want that. Penny has been mine for such a small amount of time, yet I can't imagine it any other way.

"We'll get in and out. Okay?" She squeezes my hand.

"Yeah."

It doesn't take long for someone to notice me, and it's a douche nonetheless. The guy exudes asshole and corners us in the canned soup aisle. "Gunner Dreven buying some tomato soup." He eyes the can in my hand. "No shit. What a small world."

The fact that I live, practice, and play a couple of miles from this store every day of my life doesn't make it a small world at all. But I don't bother to correct the guy. "Hey, man." I give him a nod.

"My girlfriend is a huge fan of yours. She's going to be so jealous." He pulls out his phone and initiates some selfies. It's awfully bold of him not to ask but I smile for his pictures anyway. "So we have to talk about your performance last week. Those last two should've been easy saves."

There's nothing I love more than listening to some idiot in a grocery store give me playing advice.

No doubt sensing my agitation, Penny steps between me and the guy. "Sorry, we have to go. It was nice meeting you."

"Bitch, I'm not talking to you, and I'm not done talking to Dreven. Move." He takes hold of Penny's upper arm and pushes her to the side. She stumbles off-balance and falls into the cans of soup.

I see fucking red. Before I know it, my fist is hitting the man's face.

"What the fuck?" he screeches from the ground, holding his nose. Blood drips from his fingers. "You are so done, asshole."

I squat down and move my face an inch away from his. Through gritted teeth, I seethe, "Come after me, I don't care. Don't you ever lay a hand on a woman again. If I so much as hear a whisper from you, I will make sure everyone knows that you pushed my girl."

"You're a dick, and you play like shit!" he yells as I turn away from him.

"Are you okay?" I take Penny's hand in mine, ignoring the insults spewing from the man.

She yanks her hand from mine, her face red and eyes wide. "Let's go."

We leave the store empty-handed. Penny doesn't say a word as I drive the few blocks to her house. I pull into her drive and turn off the car.

She breaks her silence. "I can't."

I turn in my seat. "You can't what?"

Her head moves from side to side. She presses her lips in a tight line. Her eyes fill with unshed tears as she says, "I can't do this with you."

"Do what?"

"A relationship, Gunner. It's over. It was stupid to even try."

Her words shock me, pulling the air from my lungs. "Wait. You're ending us? Over that prick?"

She unbuckles her seat belt and wipes the palms of her hands over her pants before turning to face me. "I'm ending us because of you. I can't be with someone who punches random guys in the soup aisle at a grocery store. That isn't normal, Gunner! I get the guy was a jerk, but you can't just punch everyone you don't like. You have no control over yourself sometimes, and I need to be with someone in control. You're..." She doesn't finish that sentence, and I have a feeling I wouldn't want to know what she was going to say anyway.

"He pushed you!" I roar. "He doesn't get to put his hands on you!"

"I can take care of myself, Gunner! What I can't do is deal with your outbursts."

"You can't end this." I shake my head in disbelief.

She takes hold of the door handle and pulls. "I already did." She steps out of the car. "I'll bring your stuff to work tomorrow," she says before slamming the door.

Mouth agape, I watch as she walks away from me and enters her house. I have no words. I'm often a man of few words, but Penny has taken them all.

I'm speechless. What just happened?

My hands ball into fists, and my head falls back against the headrest.

I should leave, pull out of this driveway right now, and depart with the shred of dignity I have left, but I can't. I'm unable to move or think or do anything but try to wrap my mind around what just happened and what it means for my future.

One without Penny in my life.

CHAPTER
TWENTY-THREE

PENNY

I school my features, plastering on the scowl—the widely used mask I've worn my whole life, and hurry toward my door. Once inside my house, I close and lock my door and fall against it. The hard wood hits my back as the tears start to fall.

Pressing a palm to my chest, I try to ease the pain of my breaking heart as tears roll down my cheeks. This is so stupid. We weren't serious. It's not like he was my soulmate or something, not that I believe in those. Gunner is and always has been a hotheaded hockey player. Nothing more. A three-day romp in Vancouver, a hot date in a closet at an animal shelter, and a month of dating does not a forever make. This was bound to end. I knew it. He knew it. Everyone knew it. Neither of us is relationship material. We tried, giving it a valiant go. This was always going to be the final result.

I just didn't expect it to hurt this much.

A heavy fist hits my door, causing me to yelp. The wood vibrates against my back, and I step away from the door. Ugh. "Go away, Gunner. I'm done talking about it!"

The pounding continues. *Bang. Bang. Bang.* A relentless rhythm that I know won't stop.

I swipe my hand across my cheeks in an attempt to dry the tears.

"Go away!" I shout.

More pounding.

With my hands on my hips, I pull a deep breath into my lungs and then slowly release it. "He can't make anything easy," I grumble to myself while turning the deadbolt of the door before opening it.

Before I can get a word out, he's inside my foyer. "Gunner, don't make this harder than it has to be. There's nothing to talk about. We're just not compatible. This doesn't have to be messy." I sigh.

"Bullshit." He storms into the living room, leaving me standing alone in the foyer.

I close the door and follow him.

"This isn't over," he insists.

"Gunner..."

He shakes his head and rolls his shoulders back.

Fierce emotion radiates from his body, but I can't quite place it...maybe, anger or regret. Longing? Everything about him is throwing me off. He's out of control but not in a threatening way. It's different from his usual bouts with anger. He seems almost emotionally unhinged.

"You know what? Fuck you, Penelope Stellars, for making me love you and then leaving me without so much as a discussion."

The love bomb throws me off and softens my resolve, but I know what I want in this life, and it's not someone who punches a man in the grocery store. "I'm sorry, Gunner. I am, but I can't be with someone—"

He cuts me off. "Yeah, I heard you the first time. But I can't stand by and watch a man put his hands on you. Don't you get that?"

"In case you haven't noticed, I'm perfectly capable of taking care of myself, Gunner. I don't need protection, and I certainly don't want that." I wave toward the door, indicating the scene we left in the store.

"He. Touched. You." Each word is a staccato.

"I know, and I'm fine." I hold my palms up and shrug.

"He touched you." This time, his words are softer and half broken. "He touched you." His words are barely a whisper, and they're coated in a deep pain.

He takes a seat on the sofa and leans his elbows

against his knees as he cradles his face in his palms. He drags his hands through his hair, and tears begin to fall. I've never seen Gunner cry, and everything in me wants to go to him, but I wait.

Looking at the floor, he clears his throat. "My mom, she...uh, had a way of picking men. I mean, she always picked the worst one available. I don't know, it was like a... sick talent. There could be a line of ten men, nine of them perfectly kind, and she'd pick the asshole. A constant stream of men came in and out of our lives when I was young and not one of them was decent. They all... uh, hit her. A lot. And believe it or not, I was this incredibly scrawny kid. I looked years younger than I was without an ounce of muscle on me. She protected me from her boyfriends by offering herself up as their punching bag. I was told to be invisible, and I was."

"Gunner," I say his name on an exhale, and he keeps his eyes on the floor but holds up a hand, gesturing for me to stay where I am.

He continues. "I wanted to protect her, you know? More than anything, I wanted to save her." He swallows. "But I... I was just so small. Always so small." His tears fall freely now against the wood floor. "I was constantly angry as a kid, and I tried to fight back and protect her. My mom didn't have much, but what she had, she used to put me into hockey. She thought it'd help with my anger and channel my behavior into something good. I loved it. It got me away from my house, and pouring my energy into something positive felt good. I was what they call a late bloomer. The summer I went away to college, I began growing like crazy. I started on my college hockey team as a forward because I was quick, but I got big and became more suited for goalie. I thought this was my chance. I spent extra time in the weight room bulking up. I had plans to go home after freshman year and remove the piece of trash dating my mother. I could finally do it. I could protect her."

His back heaves with a sob, and he runs his palms over his jean-clad thighs. I've never seen Gunner so vulnerable. It's breaking my heart.

"Only." His voice cracks. "She didn't make it to the end of my freshman year. The autopsy ruled it an accidental fall down a flight of stairs that broke her neck, but it wasn't accidental. It never was. Don't you see?" He lifts his face and holds me in his pained stare. "I had a chance to save her, and I was too late. It's my fault she's gone." His voice cracks along with my heart.

I rush to the sofa and sit beside him. "Look at me." I turn my body toward him and hold his face in my hands. "It is not your fault. Your mom's death is a tragedy, and it's heartbreaking, but it's not your fault."

He holds a curly lock of my hair between his thumb

and forefinger, rubbing it between his fingers. His eyes meet mine. "When I see a man put his hands on a woman, it fills me with blind rage, and I have to shut it down—usually by pounding his face in. But when I see a man put his hands on you, I see red. I wanted to kill that guy for shoving you. Believe me when I say that a single punch to the face was me showing restraint. I can't let him or anyone hurt you. I can't." His voice shakes on the last two words. "I know you're strong and can take care of yourself, but I need to protect you. I don't know how it happened, but against all odds, I've fallen in love with you, Pen. I won't let anything happen to you."

"Oh, Gunner." My thumb slides across the short stubble on his face. "I love you, too. This is all crazy... me and you. I'm not certain we're even compatible." I let out a dry chuckle. "Look, I get where you're coming from, I really do, but you have to understand that I grew up with someone who was always out of control. I can't live like that. I need a man who is steady and calm. I can't worry about you punching someone every time we're out in public. You make me feel cherished, and I know you'd always protect me. But I don't need you to protect me from others. I need you to protect me from chaos. I have to live in a space that is calm and serene. If I'm always waiting for the other shoe to drop and for you to go off on someone, I won't ever be truly happy. Growing up with an alcoholic does a number on you. I spent my life feeling anxious, waiting for her to explode or embarrass me or randomly throw a chair through the window of our local ice cream parlor... and yes, that happened." I give him a sad smile.

"I'll do better. I'll do anything. I'll go to therapy and anger management sessions... whatever I can do to prove to you that it won't happen again. I want to be the person you can trust. I can protect you from chaos."

"Gunner."

"I can. I promise you that I can. We're good together, Penny."

"I know." A grin tugs at my lips.

"You make me happier than I've ever been."

I nod. "Same."

"So I love you, and you love me, and we're both happy. So? Let's try."

I thread my fingers through his short hair and lock them together behind his head. "We're a mess."

"Good. Let's be a mess together." He pauses before adding, "In a calm and serene environment, of course."

I laugh. "Okay."

"Yeah?" He smiles.

"Yeah. As a side note, this is the most you've ever spoken in one sitting."

"Well, when my girl threatens to leave me, I get chatty."

My brows furrow. "I think I did leave you, though."

He shakes his head. "No, it was just a threat in a heated moment. You didn't mean it."

I chuckle. "Do we really have a chance of making it? We're quite damaged, you and I."

"That's why I know we'll make it. Our broken pieces together make us whole. We were inevitable. Even when I thought I hated you, I wanted you. I had one fucking wish, and it was you. I wished for you."

"You did?"

"Yeah, our surprise birthday party after you'd scolded me for something I didn't do. Iris had us blow out the candles and make a wish. My traitorous subconscious wished for you before I could halt the thought. It threw me off, and I didn't understand it at the time. And maybe we don't believe in soulmates and destiny and all that, but the far recesses of my mind knew I needed you before I did. A part of me has always needed you, wanted you, loved you... I just had to see it. I think apart, we may be broken, but together, we're strong. Together, we're healed."

"Who knew you were such a sweet talker?" I press my lips to his.

"Not me. I've learned a lot about myself recently."

"You and me both." I kiss him again. "Are you hungry? I guess we're ordering in after all."

"Oh, I'm very hungry." He stands from the sofa.

"But the ordering will have to wait." He picks me up and throws me over his shoulder.

I giggle as he carries me to my bedroom. I've heard that makeup sex is the best. I've never loved someone enough to make up in the first place. As is with most experiences with Gunner, this is a first. And I'm sure I'll love every second of it.

CHAPTER
TWENTY-FOUR

GUNNER

I can without a doubt say that I have never wanted anything more than I want this win. This isn't just a game. It's the determining game in the Stanley Cup finals, but it's more than that. This feels like the culmination of everything I've worked for my entire life.

It proves that all the blood, sweat, and sacrifice have meant something. That all that I lost has meant something. Happiness is at the tip of my fingertips. It seems that at thirty-three years old, my life is finally taking shape. I'm in my first serious relationship with the girl of my dreams. I feel content and at ease within my soul for the first time. Every time I've stepped on the ice, I've worn my mother's birthdate on my chest. Since I was eighteen years old, she's been here with me, and all these years later, I'm so close to the ultimate victory.

This shadow has always hovered over me, darkening my life. As much as I've tried, I've never been able to break free of it. At this moment, the light beyond—the freedom, the life, the girl are all within my reach. More than that, the forgiveness and acceptance of things I cannot change swell within my chest.

Maybe it's silly to think that the outcome of a hockey game holds any real significance over my life. But to me—it just does. It's not just a game. It's my life, and I'm ready to win.

It also seems fitting that this pivotal game in my life is against the Vancouver team that in a very real way was the catalyst for this shift. Vancouver started it all. It gave me Penny, and through her, I felt what it meant to live and feel and love.

No, the loss of this game wouldn't mean the end of my current state of happiness, but a win would bring me a level of closure that I've been craving. Absent-mindedly, my gloved hand taps the twenty-nine on my chest.

This is for you, Mom.

My gaze darts to the stands, where Penny wears a pair of tight jeans and my number twenty-nine jersey on her chest. Her long curls bounce as she jumps up and down, cheering. I've loved two women in my life. Only two. And I've loved them with everything I am.

The game is tied at two. These final seconds will determine everything. This is our chance. Vancouver is in possession now, and their hotshot center works the puck across the ice. I take in every move and every glance. Hockey is a dance of not only the body but also the mind. There's an art to the way the puck slides across the ice. The players' bodies lean to this side or that, hinting at their next move. Minute clues can be found in their glances and the angles of their sticks. Every good player tries to hide them, but there are always tells if one looks hard enough.

My job is to find them. To know where the puck is going to go before it's shot. I'm fast, but a well-shot puck is faster. If I want to stop it, I have to know where it's going.

I study the movements as the players speed down the ice. There's enough time for each team to have one more possession before the clock runs out. This puck can't get through, or in the best-case scenario, we tie.

No, this has to end now.

This is our time.

Our team has fought for this.

The Vancouver center and forward pass the puck in a well-rehearsed display. They're good—I'll give 'em that—but they're not us.

Their right forward flicks his eyes to the left corner of the net. The look happens so fast that I'm not positive it happened at all, but I trust my instincts. Their center fakes a pass to the left, pulling our guard's attention, and slaps the puck to the right forward. Without a moment's hesitation, he hits the puck toward the far left corner of the net. The puck whizzes through the space between us. Before it was hit, however, I was already diving in that direction, and my gloved hand hits the puck back onto the ice.

The hometown crowd roars. The entire area shakes in celebration, and with my part done, my teammates take over. Cade and Beckett lock in as only the two of them can. The seconds tick by. There's a pass to Beckett, a quick maneuver on his part, and then he's slapping the puck toward the net of the Vancouver goalie. Only, this time, it goes in, and the buzzer sounds.

We've won!

Chaos erupts as the entire area explodes in celebration.

A blur of navy-and-white jerseys charge to the center of the ice. I holler and join the huddle of celebration. We're a collection of cheers, hugs, tears, and genuine smiles.

We're Stanley Cup champions. We did it. These men are more than teammates. They're family, and winning with them makes it that much more sweet.

Beckett holds the metal cup over his head and skates around the ice.

This is the best moment of my life.

The enthusiastic celebration ensues as my team-mates hop around in a huddle cheering.

Time passes in a blur but slows to a halt when I see her standing by the penalty box. I skate over and pull Penny into my arms. Her warmth and sweet smell do something to my emotional resolve, and tears flow as I hold her in my arms.

"You did it, babe. I'm so proud of you. So very proud. You deserve this, Gunner. I'm so happy for you." Her voice shakes as she cries. She hugs me back with a fierce intensity, and I feel nothing but love.

"I love you, Pen."

"I love you. I'm just so happy for you."

"Thank you for being here. Thank you for loving me." The words, raw and full of emotion, fall from my lips, but I don't try to stop them. I want her to know. "This wouldn't be the same without you." I hold my gloved hand against my chest. "The twenty-ninth is my mom's birthday. I want you to know that I'm all in. With you. Forever."

The most beautiful smile crosses her face, and she cradles my face in her hands. "You should win the Stanley Cup more often," she teases. "And I know.

Forever." She pulls my face to hers, and I kiss her with everything I have.

The team parties late into the night. The bar is packed with navy-and-white jerseys, cheers, and smiles. It's been way too long since this organization has brought home the Cup. These fans deserve this win. This team deserves this win. These men, my family... we've worked so hard—training longer and harder than any other team out there—it feels so good.

The only person missing from this celebration is Beckett, and I wish he were here, especially given how much he's given to this team and his amazing shot that won us the game. But he's at the hospital welcoming his firstborn into the world, and that's pretty epic. It doesn't get better than becoming a Stanley Cup winner and a father on the same day.

I want to take this energy and pure joy and bottle it up. It's intoxicating.

Looking to my side, I see Penny. She's stunning in my jersey, with form-fitting jeans that hug her every curve and black-heeled boots. Her red curls bounce against her back, and she dances with Iris. And the smile she wears is my undoing. Penny, with her pulled-back hair, business suit, and scowl, is beautiful. This Penny—the one exuding nothing but happiness—is drop-dead gorgeous.

Only one thing can make this night better, and I can't wait another second.

I close the distance between us and lean into her ear. "You ready?"

"Sure! Are you? Have you celebrated enough with the guys?" she yells over the music.

I simply nod and extend my hand.

She takes it and threads her fingers through mine.

We say a round of quick goodbyes and take off for her place.

The second her front door is shut, we make quick work of removing our clothes. Clearly, I wasn't the only one waiting for this.

Cradling her face with my hands, we kiss—hard and rough—as we stumble into her bedroom. She falls back onto the bed and spreads her legs.

I growl, desperate to feel her. With an arm on either side of her, I crawl up her body.

Penny's moan as I slide into her wetness is the hottest sound I've ever heard. It drives me to the bridge of insanity, like everything about her does. Every. Fucking. Thing.

She captures my stare. Her big doe eyes hold me hostage as I thrust inside her. Her long red hair splays out on the bed as her ample tits bounce as I continue my assault. She's a vision, and she's mine. My fingers splay across her soft breasts, and I squeeze her nipples between my thumb and forefinger. She raises her hips, meeting me with every thrust, allowing me to go deeper. I want to explode.

We're frantic now, our bodies pounding against each other, chasing the orgasm that we're desperate for. Penny slides a hand between her legs, and the sight of her touching herself makes me growl loudly into the room. She whimpers and cries out as her body starts to shake.

Fuck yes.

I thrust into her hard, sending her body forward, and she throws her free hand out against the bed to steady herself. Our skin slaps together. More moans. Labored breaths. Slapping skin. Desperate whimpers. Guttural sighs. Sobs of pleasure.

It's the best symphony I've ever heard, and it's ours. Only ours.

We fall over the edge together, our moans of release dancing in the heated air. My body shakes with waves of pleasure. Penny breathes heavy, her full lips parted. I fall atop her, my chest expanding, desperate for air.

I roll off her, throwing my forearm over my eyes, my body still humming from pleasure. Penny scoots toward me and kisses my chest, slick with sweat.

"That was amazing." She sighs.

"Perfect," I utter. "A perfect end to a perfect day."

CHAPTER
TWENTY-FIVE

PENNY

Gunner's big body at my side and his strong hand wrapped in mine bring me a sense of peace I've never known. He's everything I've ever needed but never knew to wish for. Today feels so much different than I thought it would. Truthfully, I thought it would hurt. I was sure my chest would ache with everything I've lost.

But it's the exact opposite.

I feel nothing but complete happiness, maybe for the first time in my life.

Tucker and Marcela's wedding was utterly beautiful. She was every bit the perfect-looking model I knew she'd be standing at the altar in her elegant form-fitting gown. He was even more handsome than he was in high school. He's grown into his skin and matured into a man. The pair could both secure modeling gigs and more than just Target. All the chain stores would take them—they're that beautiful.

While Tucker was everything I remembered him to be and more, not an ounce of remorse surfaced because he's not the man who holds my heart. He's not Gunner.

I've yet to speak to anyone from high school since Gunner and I snuck into the back of the church right before Marcela walked down the aisle and left immediately after the ceremony. But I'm not worried about seeing them all at the reception. The Penny that knew them all then had everything to prove. I realize now that I don't owe them anything. Some may judge me; others may not. But I've learned that what others think of me is none of my business. I don't live my life for them. I live it for me. Only my opinion matters. Truth be told, it's the only one that should've ever mattered. I'm glad I see that now.

Hand in hand, we ascend the stairs to the classy reception hall. Each step is flanked by a clear pink frosted glass container, resembling a small punch bowl filled with water and a floating candle. Behind each bowl is a stunning bouquet. The amount of preparation that went into the steps leading up to the reception is astounding. Atop the steps is a magnificent floral archway. The sheer sum of money spent on the parts of the reception I've seen is more than the entire budget for most of the weddings I've attended, and we've yet to step inside.

Gunner's hand squeezes mine. "You excited?"

"To hang out with every person from my graduating class and reminisce about high school. Oh, you bet. Ecstatic."

"Nervous?"

I shake my head. "No, I'm not nervous."

"You look absolutely stunning tonight." He releases his grip on my hand and turns to face me. Swiping one of my long, curly locks of hair off my face, he leans down and presses his lips to mine.

I sigh, melting into the kiss.

"We could just go," I offer once Gunner has pulled away.

"Are you kidding? With a walkway like that, the food is bound to be incredible, and I'm starving."

"True. Plus, if we leave now, I won't be able to show you off." Gunner is always sexy, but Gunner in a three-piece suit is stunning.

He grins. "I think you have that the other way around. I'll have the hottest girl in the place."

"True." I chuckle.

"I love you, Pen."

Lifting my arm, I cup his jaw with my hand. His

trimmed beard is soft against my hand, opposite to what one would think it'd be. He's so handsome, it hurts. "I love you."

He takes my hand once more and leads me inside.

"You're getting the steak, by the way," I say.

"Works for me."

We've barely entered the hall before I'm being tackled in a hug. "Pen!" Gabby shrieks.

"Hey, Gabs." I hug her back.

She releases me and looks at Gunner, her eyes going wide. "Oh my freaking God. It's the Beast! You know you're the reason I watch hockey!" She looks at me, her eyes squinting. "You're dating the Beast! How could you not tell your best friend that you're dating the hottest guy on the Crane hockey team?" she all but shrieks.

"Gunner, Gabby. Gabby, Gunner." I make the introduction.

Gabby extends her hand. "I'm the best friend."

Gunner is a perfect gentleman. "It's nice to meet you, Gabby. I've heard so much about you," he lies. The single conversation we shared about Gabby took a total of two minutes. There's not much to tell. But now that I think about how she keeps calling me her best friend, I wonder what her life is like now. Because if I'm truly her best friend, that's sad. We haven't seen each other in years. I make a mental note to talk to her more.

She turns back to me. Leaning in, she lowers her voice. "But seriously… you're dating him?"

I chuckle. "Yeah."

"Is it serious?" she questions.

Gunner answers for me. "Oh yeah."

"Oh my gosh, you are living my dream life. So lucky." She extends her arms out in front of her, gesturing toward the large reception hall. "This is something else, huh? I told you her parents had mad money."

I look around at the reception that could be, and probably is, in a wedding magazine. "Yeah, it's gorgeous."

"Tucker looks so happy, doesn't he?"

I nod with a genuine smile on my face. "He really does."

"Come on. We're at the same table." She takes my hand and leads me across the space. Looking back over her shoulder, she says, "You have to meet my date, Brian. Unlike you and Gunner, we are not serious. He's the bartender at work."

"You still at the same place?"

"Yep! Been serving at Red Robin for five years now. I love it there," she says of the burger joint chain she works for.

"Gunner and I have been obsessed with their fries lately but only with…"

"Ketchup and ranch!" Gabby finishes my sentence.

"And extra seasoning salt," I add.

"Yeah, as a server, I can get a basket of fries for free, so I swear I eat them for half my meals."

I can't help but notice she still has an amazing figure. Why some people have incredible metabolisms and others don't is beyond me. If I ate nothing but fries, I'd be a whale. But at least I'd be a sexy one. I've accepted the fact that my body is going to do what it's going to do. All that matters to me is that I feel healthy and strong. I'm grateful to my body for carrying me through this beautiful life, regardless of its shape or size.

Plus, Gunner loves my curves. In fact, he's obsessed with them.

Besides Gunner and Brian, our table consists of people who graduated from the same high school. True to many small towns, many of my classmates married and remained in the same town where we grew up. I suppose that reality is my literal hell, but to each their own.

Gunner's brilliance outshines even the fantastical surroundings of this wedding. Sometimes I forget that I'm dating a celebrity of sorts. I'm sure Gunner hates every second of the spotlight, but it works for me.

There are fewer questions I have to answer. Who cares about the PR rep for an NHL hockey team when they have the star goalie to talk to instead?

He handles the questions and attention like a pro. Taking him in as he talks to my former classmates, I feel so fortunate to call this man mine. In a very short time, he's become everything to me.

The dinner is incredible. While I originally ordered the steak entrée because it was the most expensive option, I'm glad I did. It's one of the most delicious meals I've ever eaten. I'm sure Marcela's parents hired some celebrity chef to cater this event. Heck, Bobby Flay is probably busy in the kitchen as we speak. There's not an ounce of jealousy inside me. I truly feel nothing but happiness for my first love and his Target model.

This year has changed me. Thank goodness. I needed a reality check.

I have no regrets and it feels great.

Gunner finds my leg beneath the table. His strong hand squeezes my knee before sliding up my inner thigh, and his fingers graze my skin. On instinct, my body reacts. My chest expands as I draw in a breath. Goose bumps pebble my skin, and every cell in my body instantly wants Gunner in all the ways I can get him.

Channeling every ounce of willpower, I slide my

arm beneath the table and halt his hand before shooting him what I hope is a discreet-yet-serious warning glare. While it goes against my deepest desires, I know that if I allow Gunner to do what he wants to do, I will, in fact, leave here with regrets. These people came for a dinner, not a show—at least not one starring me.

He leans in and brushes his lips over my ear before whispering, "You're no fun."

I grin and shake my head. "You promised to behave."

"I am." He supplies a peck to my neck before sitting back in his chair.

The truth is, I'm ready to go. The wedding was beautiful and the meal, heavenly. Chatting with people I haven't seen in almost a decade has been okay, but a night alone with Gunner would make me the happiest. Only, I haven't had a chance to congratulate the happy couple yet. They've been busy with bride and groom duties—the pictures, dances, and cake cutting.

I turn in my chair to face Gunner. "I don't know if I want all of this extravagance when I get married. It seems like a hassle." I clamp my lips shut when I realize I'm talking about marriage—a topic of conversation Gunner and I have yet to explore, if we don't count his declaration of forever after the Stanley Cup win, which I don't. He was so high on life that night that I can't hold him to anything he said.

My words don't seem to faze him. "No? You don't want a big wedding?"

I shake my head. "It seems like so much work. I want to enjoy the day."

"Yeah, I agree. I picture me and my wife somewhere beautiful, just the two of us, vows and endless sex."

Glass to my lips, I almost inhale the water in my mouth. "You're such a romantic," I scoff.

He raises a brow. "Oh, I guarantee you, she'll have no complaints. It will be romantic as hell."

"I never pictured you as a guy who plans his future wedding."

His shoulders rise. "I never was."

The implication that he is now causes my heart to race in my chest.

His deep brown eyes hold my stare. My tongue peeks out, licking my bottom lip before I pull my lip with my teeth. Gunner's gaze drops to my mouth, and his lips part. The desire to touch him is so intense it's almost painful, but I don't dare. If I've learned anything about us, we're not to be trusted in moments like this. Gunner makes me feral with need, and I lose my head. We're about two seconds from finding a coat closet. I need to rein this in.

"Nelly!" Tucker's voice cuts through the lust-filled haze surrounding me.

I bolt up from my chair and turn to face him. "Hey!" the greeting comes out louder than I anticipated.

"I'm so happy you made it. I want you to meet Marcela." He turns to his beautiful bride. "Babe, this is Nelly."

"Nelly." She leans in and kisses my right cheek and then my left, the greeting throws me off as does the name. Tucker is the only one who has ever used that nickname, and coming from anyone else, it grates on my nerves. "I've heard so many wonderful things about you. It's a pleasure to meet you."

"You too. Such a beautiful wedding. Thank you for having us."

Gunner is standing at my side. His arm circles around my waist.

"Gunner Dreven?" Tucker asks, his tone carries an air of disbelief.

Gunner extends his free hand. "Pleasure to meet you. Congratulations to you both."

"Wow, I didn't know you were dating the G.O.A.T goalie, Nelly," Tucker says to me before addressing Gunner. "I'm a huge fan, man. You were amazing this season. Congrats on the Cup win."

"Thank you. You and Marcela should come out for

a game. Penny can hook you up with VIP tickets anytime," Gunner says.

"No shit? You can do that?" Tucker asks me.

"Hell yeah, she can. She pretty much runs the whole Crane Organization. She can do anything," Gunner answers for me.

I feel my cheeks redden. With a shake of my head, I say, "I don't *run* the organization."

Gunner chuckles. "She basically does. She keeps us all in check."

"So you're like the boss?" Tucker questions.

"Yes." Gunner answers in unison with my, "No."

I nudge Gunner's side. "I'm not the boss. I'm head of PR and keep everything running smoothly."

"Don't let her fool you. She's the boss," Gunner states.

Tucker smiles wide. "Good for you, Nelly. I always knew you'd do incredible things. God, it's so good to see you. It's been way too long."

"It has. So tell me about you. Where are you working?" I look between Tucker and Marcela. "Where are you two living?"

Tucker tells us all about his life with Marcela. He goes on about his promotion and the new house they purchased. A smile crosses my face as he speaks. He looks genuinely happy, and it fills my heart. After a couple of minutes, Tucker says, "Well, we need to make the rounds, but it was so good catching up. Don't be a stranger, Nelly. It was great to meet you, Gunner."

"You too, and I'm serious. Hit Penny up about those tickets. We'd love to have you out for a game."

"I definitely will." Tucker smiles. He leans in and gives me a hug, whispering, "I'm happy for you, Nel."

"I'm happy for you," I whisper back, giving him a squeeze.

With that, the couple is off to chat with the next guests. My stare follows them as they move on, and moisture finds my eyes. I'm overcome with a sense of peace and gratitude. I've been dreading this day for months, and every fear I harbored was unwarranted. Not an ounce of longing is left in me for Tucker. I was genuinely happy to see him, not because he was my first love but because he was my friend. I'm so different from the girl he knew, but I realize that's a good thing. I'm better, stronger, happier. I don't feel a sliver of inadequacy. In fact, with Gunner at my side, I felt nothing but pride in who I've become.

It's a strange feeling—to watch the person you felt destined to be with—walk away with someone else and feel grateful that it's not you on his arm. A tear rolls down my cheek, and I turn to Gunner.

"I love you."

He swipes a curl behind my ear and presses his

thumb across my cheek, wiping the tear away. "I love you. Is everything okay?"

Another tear falls at the realization that I am genuinely happy for the first time in my life. The journey to this moment in time hasn't been easy. It has taken me years, but I made it, and I would do it all again to end up here. Now that I know what it is to be utterly free and joyful in one's skin, I'm never going back to the person I was. Deep down, I know that when Gunner called me his forever, Stanley Cup win or not, he meant it. There's no doubt in my mind that he's my forever, and I'm his.

This journey hasn't been only to find myself. It's been to find him. "It's better than okay. Let's get out of here."

The corners of his mouth turn up. "That's what I'm talking about."

CHAPTER
TWENTY-SIX

GUNNER

Window down, the warm August air hits my arm as I drive toward Penny's condo. There's this inexplicable peace surrounding me. This state of being is something I'd never felt until recently, until her. Getting something you never knew existed is surreal. I never knew to wish for this life because I didn't know it existed. Yet instinctively, I knew to wish for her. She's always been the key to unlocking this happiness.

Given our start and hatred toward one another, we shouldn't work. And now... I can't imagine a life without her by my side. She's the only one for me. She's quickly become my entire life. I've always felt like a lone island fighting the torrent of the sea, but no more. I have a partner in this life, and it's so much better.

I'm no longer the closed-off person I was. Penny now knows everything. We've talked at length about our pasts and the unfortunate similarity that ties us together—the trauma surrounding our mothers. I held the memories of my mother close to my chest and didn't share her existence with anyone for years. I thought giving voice to that part of my life would cause a torrent of pain that would swallow me whole. In reality, Penny has given me a safe space to share my love for my mom. Talking about her has brought peace. Denying a voice to such a big part of one's life is painful. Bringing my mother back to life through stories, both the good and the bad, has healed me when I didn't know I was broken.

To say that Penny and the love we share has saved my life isn't an understatement. Sure, without her, I would've been alive in the technical term, but I would've never known what it feels like to really *live*. Existing and living are two very separate realities, and I'm so grateful to understand the latter.

I park in Penny's drive, turn off the car, and grab the pink box from the local bakery and the Trenta-sized Starbucks coffee cup before heading inside.

"Pen!" I call out when I enter.

"In the kitchen!" she calls back, and I hear the clank of dishes being loaded into the dishwasher.

Her distraction gives me time to set the stage. I click on the TV, go to the streaming service, and start season 6, episode 25 of *Friends*—"The One with the Proposal." Is this a whole new level of cheese? Yes, it is. But, I've always been a go big or go home kind of guy, and if I'm leaning into the romantic cheese, I'm diving in headfirst and slathering that shit everywhere. I do mute it, however, because while it helps to set the stage —it's not the main event.

Penny enters the living room. Her mouth opens to speak, but she closes it, doing a double take of her favorite show on the television. "What is…" she starts to ask, her voice trailing off when she focuses in on me standing on the other side of the room, a small cake box in one hand and a cup of coffee in the other.

A wide smile graces her beautiful face, and she skips over to me. "You brought me coffee?"

I hold out the large paper cup. "Not just any coffee."

She takes a sip, and her eyes bulge. "How did you get your hands on a PSL? They don't release for eight days!"

"I have my ways." I supply a smug smirk. To be fair, it wasn't easy getting her a pumpkin spiced latte early. It required Iris's friend who works at our local Starbucks and her connection to the store manager, a bit of begging on my part, and VIP tickets to a home game for the manager and his friends, along with a thousand-dollar tip. But I would've done anything to get her this cup of coffee. "And I got you a present." I hold out the pink box.

She sets the coffee down on the mantel of the fireplace. "What is this all for?"

"It's August sixteenth. Our half birthday."

She chuckles. "We celebrate our half birthday?"

"We do now." I smile.

"You are the sweetest." She takes the box from me and opens the lid. She gasps, her eyes filling with tears.

Inside the box are two frosted donuts with sprinkles. There is a candle in each donut, and wrapped around one of the candles is a platinum, three-carat diamond halo cushion-cut engagement ring.

Her mouth falls open in a gasp, and I take the box back from her to retrieve the ring. I set the donuts on the mantel next to her coffee and drop to one knee.

"My beautiful Penelope." I hold the ring out to her. "Six months ago, my heart made a wish, and at that time, I didn't even know exactly what I was wishing for, but I saw you. You have always been the answer. I often wonder why it took so long for me to see that, but I think I couldn't see it until I was ready for all the beautiful experiences you've brought to my life. I am so grateful to you for finding me, the real me, and loving me for who I am with all my baggage. I never knew that life could be like this, and now that I do, I will fight for the rest of my life to keep it, to keep you and love you and make you the happiest woman in the world. Will you please marry me?"

Tears course down her cheeks, and the most beautiful smile crosses her face. She nods enthusiastically. "Yes, Gunner. Of course I will marry you." She falls to her knees, wraps her arms around my neck, and pulls me in for a hug. Our lips meet, and the kiss is wet from tears and messy from our collective smiles and laughter—and absolutely fucking perfect.

I break the kiss and take her hand. Her hand trembles as I slide the ring on her finger. "Do you like it?"

"Are you kidding? It's perfect. It's so me."

"I thought it was the perfect ring for you."

She holds her hand out in front of her, the diamond sparkling on her hand. "It is. Oh my God," she shrieks. "I can't believe this!"

"Oh wait." I stand and retrieve the donuts. I pull out the white cardboard tray from the bottom of the box that holds the donuts and retrieve a lighter from my pocket.

Penny stands. "What are you doing?"

"I have a whole plan." I light the candles.

"You are the cutest. All of my favorite things are in

one room—*Friends*, coffee, and you." She holds out her hand and admires her ring once more. "And added to that list are now sprinkled donuts and this ring." She grins.

I hold the candle lit donuts between us. "Something started in February when we blew out those candles, and then in Vancouver when you brought me the stale sprinkled donuts on our birthday just like the ones my mom used to bring me. I've never believed in fate and all that, but I do now. We came together despite all odds and our stubborn nature. The universe brought us together, forcing us in that god-awful hotel room. Everything that happened was a sign until so many signs were shoved in my face that I couldn't ignore my path to happiness anymore. You are my happiness, Pen. I would burn the entire world down for you."

She shakes her head, fresh tears falling. "I don't need you to burn the world for me, Gunner. I just need you to walk by my side through this life and love me."

"I will always love you."

"And that is all I will ever need from you."

The candles, half their original size, flicker between us. "To my future Mrs. Dreven, it is time to make a wish."

She presses her lips into a smile and closes her eyes, visualizing her wish, and then we blow out the candles together. My wish is the same one I made in February.

Only this time, I'm not confused or hesitant. I'm a hundred percent sure. I see her face in bright, vivid color.

And the wish is less of a wish and more of a thank-you because everything I needed has already come true.

I found the love of my life, and she's just agreed to be mine.

CHAPTER
TWENTY-SEVEN

PENNY

Vancouver hits different in the summer. It's still a beautiful city, but it's not the same without the death-defying snowstorm and staying in a musty room equipped for toilet paper storage.

Sliding my hands over my mop of curls, I put it in a side ponytail as Gunner speeds down the country road that leads back into the city. The sun shines bright as we pass mountains blanketed in evergreens. Driving a Jeep with its soft cover top off is not good for my hair or my skin. I pull my light jacket over my shoulders.

"Cold?" Gunner questions.

"No. Trying not to get burnt. I don't want to spend our honeymoon in pain."

"Damn. Sorry, babe. I keep forgetting I'm married

to a ginger." He chuckles. "Maybe this wasn't the best choice of vehicles."

I look at Gunner and his perfectly tanned skin. "It's okay. It's easy for those with the ability to tan to forget." The statement isn't said in anger but truth. Those who weren't born with pale skin don't realize the torture that is the sun. "At least we're north and not honeymooning in the Caribbean or something. If we were there, I'd be doing nothing but swimming in sunscreen." I turn to the side and lean my face against the headrest, taking in my gorgeous husband. "It was nice to see Frank and Alice, wasn't it?"

"Yeah, it was." He smiles. "They're like family, almost. You know?"

I nod. "Well, they played an important role in our life. They didn't seem surprised when we told them we were married."

"No, they didn't."

"Come to think of it, most of the people we know weren't shocked at all."

"I guess they saw something we were too stubborn to see."

"True." I absentmindedly rub the ring on my finger. I can't get enough of it. I've only worn it for a week, but feeling the weight on my finger makes me so happy.

Gunner and I wasted no time getting married. The

day after he proposed, we applied for our marriage license and married two days later in the courthouse. It was a simple ceremony with Iris and Cade as our witnesses. Now, we're on our honeymoon in the place it all started for us.

I was serious when I said I didn't want the pomp and circumstance of a big, elaborate wedding. Heck, I didn't even want the minimal effort required to plan a backyard wedding. I spend my days attached to my calendar, planning events for a living. I wanted a marriage that was effortless… just me and him. No coordinating with vendors, invites to be sent, decisions on colors or cakes to be made—none of it. All that matters is that Gunner is mine, and I am his.

Thankfully, he wanted the same.

I'm sure Iris will plan a dinner with our Crane family to celebrate when we get back, and we're cool with that because we're already married.

We could've waited a bit to marry, but neither of us saw the point. It's hard to wait to start your forever, so we didn't. I don't have a doubt in my mind about this marriage. It was all very… kismet. Who knows? It could've been our mothers in heaven pulling the strings and orchestrating it all. Everything happened the way it needed to happen to bring us together. There's no doubt that a greater power was at play. The how doesn't matter as much as the now. My now—this life with Gunner—is everything.

I truly never thought I'd get this lucky or be this happy.

"What did it feel like being back in that room again?" I ask, remembering the curious looks on Frank's and Alice's faces when we asked to revisit our previous quarters.

The glorified storage closet where we were holed up for three days was the same as it was last winter. The only difference was the lack of snowdrifts against the windows. The same chaotic piles of boxes, musty smell, and one double-sized bed were exactly as I remembered.

"Honestly?" he huffs out a laugh. "That room made me horny as hell."

Giggles explode, and I nod my head. "Same. What is wrong with us?"

He shrugs. "We had some great times in that room. Had we not, we wouldn't be here now."

"I know. I almost wanted to ask to stay there. *Almost.*"

"Just hold on to that feeling for a few more minutes, and I'll make you forget all about that room." He reaches his hand over and rubs my thigh. My body immediately tingles.

He's right. Our chemistry is an inferno, no matter where we are. The penthouse suite overlooking the city of Vancouver and the beautiful blue water below is a much better spot for a romantic honeymoon. But the dingy little motel room will always hold fond memories.

The only plans I made surrounding these nuptials was this honeymoon. With a quick Google search, I made a list of some fun summer activities we could do here in Vancouver, and Gunner booked the suite.

True to form, once we get back to the hotel, we don't leave our suite until we fly back to Michigan. We don't explore the city at all or experience any of the activities I planned. We remain in our room wrapped up in one another for the entire week. Much like our first stay in Vancouver, we communicate with few words, but our bodies feel everything. Admittedly, the accommodations are better this time. There's no cardboard smell, and the room service is phenomenal.

Our stay in that motel back in February will always hold a special place in my heart. But this stay takes the cake. Because this time, when we check out, I won't lose him or this connection. This time, when he brings my body to ultimate satisfaction, he does so completely in love with me as I am with him.

Chemistry is great, but love is everything.

With Gunner, I have both.

And I always will.

Dear Readers,

You finally got Gunner and Penny's story! Yay! I know this book was quite delayed. This year has been something else. So many things have been happening in my life that have pulled attention from my writing, and I'm sorry it took longer than anticipated to get this out. But I am so happy with the way Gunner and Penny's story turned out, and I hope you love it as much as I do! Thank you so much for all the love for *One Pucking Love* and *One Pucking Heart* while you waited for this book—especially to my Tiktok community. I love you all so much! You have been supportive and excited about this series and understanding *One Pucking Wish's* delay. Your kind messages and comments have filled my heart. I am truly so grateful for you all.

To all my readers, without you, I wouldn't be able to have my dream job. Everyday, I'm just so grateful that this is my life. I've always been a storyteller and a hopeless romantic. Thank you for allowing me to share these stories and for loving them the way that you do!

I love this hockey romance life and adore the characters in the Crane Hockey Series. It brings me so much joy to write these books. So much so, that what was going to be a four-book series is now going to be a six-book series. Now that Cade, Beckett, and Gunner have found their HEAs (happily ever afters), it's time for Sebastian (Bash), Jaden, and Max to get theirs. The next three books entitled, *One Pucking Destiny*, *One Pucking Chance*, and *One Pucking Life* are coming soon, and I can't wait for you to read them!

Don't forget to download your free Christmas Bonus Epilogue for Penny and Gunner (It's a hot one!). Information is available in the link in my bio on all social media platforms.

Or here...

https://linktr.ee/authorelliewade

Enjoy!

I've said this many times, but this is a hard job. In truth, it's the most difficult job I've ever had, yet I love it so much. I love writing love stories with flawed characters who have to work for their HEA. Thank you for reading so I can continue to write.

Thank you for every social media post share or comment, every message, review, or recommendation to your book friends. It all matters, and it all gives authors the fuel to keep going in a very brutal industry. I truly can't express just how grateful I am to every single one of you.

Make your life a beautiful one.

Forever,

Ellie <3

LET'S CONNECT!

Readers—You can connect with me on several places, and I would love to hear from you.

Join my readers group: www.facebook.com/groups/wadeswarriorsforthehea

Find me on Facebook: www.facebook.com/Ellie WadeAuthor

Find me on Instagram: www.instagram.com/ authorelliewade

Find me on TikTok: https://www.tiktok.com/@ authorelliewade

Visit my website: www.elliewade.com

Sign up for my newsletter: https://app.mailerlite. com/webforms/landing/y8i5t2

OTHER TITLES BY ELLIE WADE

For information on Ellie's books, please visit her website.

www.elliewade.com

The Choices Series

A Beautiful Kind of Love

A Forever Kind of Love

A Grateful Kind of Love

The Flawed Heart Series

Finding London

Keeping London

Loving London

Eternally London

Taming Georgia

The Beautiful Souls Collection

Bared Souls

Kindred Souls

Captivated Souls

Fated Souls

Destined Souls

Entwined Souls

The Crane Hockey Series

One Pucking Love

One Pucking Heart

One Pucking Wish

One Pucking Destiny

One Pucking Chance

One Pucking Life

The Heroes of Fire Station Twelve

Fragment

Found

Fated

Standalones

Forever Baby

Chasing Memories

A Hundred Ways to Love

Box Sets

The Flawed Heart Series

The Choices Series

Soul Mates

The Beautiful Souls Collection

The Beauty in the Journey Collection

Crane Hockey

Cherry Blossom Grove

Ellie Wade's Sweet Collection

Licorice Wishes

ABOUT THE AUTHOR

Ellie Wade resides in southeast Michigan with her husband, three children, and three dogs. She loves the beauty of her home state, especially the lakes and the gorgeous autumn weather. When she is not writing, you will find her reading, hanging out with her kids, or spending time with family and friends. She loves traveling and exploring new places with her family.